Ray DiZazzo

Moonmare
A Science Fiction Novel

Granite-Collen

Published by
Granite-Collen Communications
PO Box 621
Camarillo, CA 93011

This is a work of fiction. All names, characters and incidents are
products of the author's imagination. Any resemblance or connection to actual persons, living or dead, events or locations is
strictly coincidental.

Printed in the United States of America

ISBN: 0-9648-8003-2
ISBN-13: 9780964880030

DEDICATION

This book is dedicated to Mac and
Cedric McKelvey, my wife Patti, and those
who battle abuse in its many forms, especially
the abuse of children, animals
and senior citizens.

MOONRUNNER

27 tons, eleven legs
resembling a giant fetal mare
aboard a caravan of sows,
she is moving lunar south
loping in the silver dust.

Her mouths are crackling
on either temple, talking inward
chirruping into coils and recorders.

Through her face, oblong, gelatal
the constellations sail, sparkling
in webs of membrane.

We, the gibbous Earth, gliding now
above her back, gleaming on the plaques:

one of UNON, one
of the American Flag.

> — *Clovin's Head*
> Red Hill Press, 1976

ONE

Sound cannot exist in a vacuum.

Had an atmosphere thick enough to carry sound waves enveloped the moon, for the first 4 billion years of its existence it would have given voice to the natural growing pains of celestial evolution: The intermittent creaking of shifting ground plates, volcanic rumblings, the bubbling of molten lava and blasts of escaping steam, the whistle of incoming meteors followed by the quakes from their impacts, and the ensuing rain of metallic fragments dropping with gentle puffs into the dusty lunar soil.

On one night, in the year 1969, a new and completely unnatural succession of "would be" sounds came to the moon's vacuum. The first began as a rumble high in the stars. Slowly strengthening, it grew into the roar of a descending earth-made spacecraft - a geometric hunk of metal on tubular legs, wrapped in what looked like gold tinfoil and stamped with an American flag.

Reaching ground level, Eagle's blast died away with the heavy impact of its landing pods.

Immediately, things began moving around inside the metal hull. Faint thumps preceded the mechanical whine of hydraulic arms, the rotation of video camera lenses, and the scarcely audible static of radio transmissions. Following this came the sudden hiss of escaping oxygen and the metal clank of an opening hatch. Finally, a large boot stepped onto a metal ladder. With another step, a man-made sole placed the first alien footprint on lunar ground.

From that moment forward, over the next four decades, thousands of new, unnatural, and unheard sounds came to many places on the moon: Radios, car engines, shovel blades slicing into the grey soil, picks splitting dirt clumps, concrete pouring, wrenches tightening, walls being hoisted, the ratcheting of nuts and bolts, drills coring rock, human voices, hydraulic arms lifting and carrying and, of course, the incessant comings and goings of earth-made spacecraft.

On this night, again, it was something new - a metal hexagonal cylinder the approximate size of a large section of storm drain. The object came down slowly out of the lunar night on the upward force of four jets. Approaching ground level at a place on the moon that faces perpetually away from the earth, it hovered for nearly thirty seconds.

At a moment calculated months earlier, small jet engines near each end and along the sides of the cylinder fired a concert of tiny, computer timed blasts. The craft wobbled and yawed as if dangling on an invisible string. Having swung lunar west exactly 32 degrees, the cross-hairs on a spotter scope mounted on the craft's head end fell into exact alignment with the star Pollux. The craft stopped and held at this position for three seconds. Again, the jets fired. This sequence corrected the cylinder's pitch, roll and yaw, making it perfectly level with the surface below. With this accomplished, the main engines wound slowly down and the object settled onto the surface on its six pod feet.

Once down, an assortment of preprogrammed functions began immediately. The aft end of the cylinder neatly unhinged exposing a curled hydraulic arm on which were multiple layers of solar battery panels. The arm uncurled, the panels rotated, fanned out into four circular faces, and the entire arrangement settled into the lunar soil facing the sky.

The sun was close to setting.

Now motionless, the craft generated nothing that would have created any sound on any moon with an atmosphere for the next fourteen hours.

TWO

Muriel Olsen was relieved to see the nearly two hundred students that filled Forum Class 7-A begin clearing their desktops and loading books into their backpacks.

"Before next week," she said into her headset microphone, "Chapters 7 and 11 in Millersen." Having said this, she paused, looking out over the groups of students, many now getting to their feet. Her comment seemed to have been ignored. "And since I know you've all been so busy you've already gotten most of that reading done," she continued, "I'd like a first draft of your edited interview transcripts as well."

With this statement a collective moan rose from the class of Poli-Sci students who now began making their way down the aisles of the huge theater classroom toward the exits.

Better, Muriel thought.

In some odd way it pleased her to know her students were leaving at least a little depressed. There were too many drug and beer parties these days, too many "ragers" and "raves" and "dorm storms". Too much sex and apathy and too many expensive cars. A small dose of real world hopelessness was in order.

She began packing her books and curricula. She cleared the podium and a nearby work table, then turned off and stored away the laptop that shortly before had been showing images of the House and Senate in session. She stepped down from her podium, and with an arm load of books and papers, made her way to the door.

Leaving the classroom she walked a short distance to an elevator. She stepped in, noting the lingering smell of cologne and stale cigarette smoke, and rose two floors. Exiting, she walked along a series of short linoleum hallways, eventually arriving at a door on which was a small, worn plastic name plaque that read "Dr. Muriel Olsen – Governmental Studies".

She inserted her key in the lock, entered the small, brick-walled office and, as she reached her desk, dropped the load of books and materials into a chair. Several phone messages had been taken by her student assistant. Muriel began leafing through them and two quickly caught her eye. The first was a reminder of her appointment later in the week with Dr. Cynthia Weil. Muriel winced slightly as she read this one, but the next message immediately changed her expression. For the first time that day, she smiled. The call had been from Jack, and it requested her call back. She looked at her wristwatch. 2:34. He would be at his desk doing his afternoon paperwork. She removed her bulky tweed sweater, rolled up her sleeves and dialed.

Her call was answered by Lieutenant Colonel Jack Moore at Barton Air Force Base. At fifty-two, Moore was nearly ten years older than Muriel. He was handsome and fit, with thick black hair, brilliant blue eyes and a tall muscular frame. Just as Muriel had guessed, he was seated behind a small, worn desk signing requisitions. He worked in a neat but sterile military office, and to-day, as on most office days, he was in khaki dress.

"Hi!" Muriel said.

Jack smiled. "I had a great idea."

Muriel rolled her eyes and chuckled. "What now?" she asked.

"This weekend. First, on Saturday, the Space Museum. There's a new display on black holes. Then the Telecom Software Expo on Sunday. You'll love 'em both. Trust me."

As he was saying this, Jack reached into his center desk drawer and removed a small, burgundy, felt covered box. He opened it and smiled, gazing down at a full carat diamond engagement ring.

Meanwhile, Muriel had quickly shoveled through her books and papers and found her calendar. She opened it, flipped a few pages, and verified what she could have told Jack from the start - the weekend was wide open. "Sounds great!" she said. Then she became serious. "...I miss you!"

Jack paused. He looked again at the diamond ring and said, "Me too."

THREE

On the fifteenth hour after the craft had landed, eleven tiny step motors suddenly came to life. A series of whirring, split-second bursts of air pressure "popped" at several places on the craft. These activated small hydraulic arms that quickly raised and rotated a group of six dark, outer panels on the cylinder. The panels locked into vertical positions like chrome, rectangular wall boards held up to the stars on white insect arms.

These movements revealed six areas of translucent, brownish, window-like surfaces on the landing craft, and in the same motion set in place the additional solar panels needed to power the remainder of the craft's many internal functions.

Moments after the panel motors had stopped, a new group started up. These, too, ran for only a few moments. They stopped when six bottom panels dropped from the underbelly of the cylinder, exposing a shiny, less than paper-thin sheet. The material left exposed was Galvonex-EL, a metallic, extremely thin, high-strength membrane that allowed single molecules of oxygen to pass through it at a very slow and precisely calculable rate. With its exposure to the lunar environment, the process had begun which, over a period of fifty-six hours, would allow all oxygen to escape from the cylinder and create a vacuum inside.

It was during that same period of time that the translucent top "windows" would slowly lose their dense brownish color, fading to a completely transparent covering over the large, barely visible, organism inside.

Documenting this process were two digital meters built into the head end of the craft, adjacent to its spotter scope. The meter representing the translucency of the brownish surfaces on top of the cylinder was labeled "LT EXP". Its current reading was 000.001%, and it was rising at a very slow rate. The meter representing the oxygen level in the craft was labeled "OXYG". It's current reading was 099.999%. It was slowly dropping.

FOUR

Nearly three earth days after the countdown had begun, the readings on the digital meters had reversed. The meter labeled "LT EXP" read 099.999%. The one labeled "OXYG" read 000.001%. Minutes later, the readings went to 100% and 0% respectively. The organism inside the craft remained perfectly still.

In the sixty-third hour a large, multi-stranded cluster of braided cords that had previously been connected to the organism by a fitting that looked similar to a huge, gold pipe coupler, popped free. Its locking seal had ruptured from the pressure created by the now vacuum state inside the craft. This release triggered a digital pulse transmission that in turn activated a powerful earth-based radio transceiver.

Several seconds after the coupling popped, Dr. Andrew Weincamp intently watched the computer that told him his transceiver had gone into operation. In the dim light of a laboratory, six stories underground in the Southern California desert, he smiled broadly and began to slowly nod his head.

Moments later he heard a pleasant tone. He quickly turned to his right and watched a second program boot up and begin to run. Under a heading which read "UMBL", its first message was:

Umbilical rupture.
Moonmare now on earth signal.

Immediately following this, a rapid stream of digital information began to scroll up on the screen. Above the information was the title:

Functions - Basic

On the moon, the hexagonal craft now performed its final operations. It began to literally blow itself apart, piece by piece, at the joints. Clusters of air blasts popped hinges, bolts unscrewed and dropped free, coiled wires and wrapped tubes fell apart, and finally, large segments of the body of the craft began falling outward onto the lunar ground. When this had been completed, all that remained was a pile of metallic rubble surrounding a large, rectangular, titanium rack that looked very similar to a huge white barbecue grill.

Lying on the rack, now fully exposed to the lunar vacuum and frigid night temperature, was the organism which had been named Moonmare. For the most part she laid perfectly still, but occasionally muscular tissue below her skin quivered like that of a dreaming animal.

Along the rail under one side of the rack was an air bag system which now went into action. As the bag inflated, the rack slowly began to lean up and tilt. Four minutes later, Moonmare rolled off onto the moon's surface. This abrupt "birth tumble" provided the same stimulation a doctor's hand might on the bottom of a newborn infant. On its sudden contact with the cold, white soil, a shudder raced through the thick, mostly black, body.

It was in response to this shock that another completely new, unheard sound now came to the moon's vacuum - the "voice" of Moonmare. Had air been present her "language" would have, at first, sounded like the hesitant warble of a tiny songbird.

Beginning slowly as a few sporadic "peeps", her "talk" quickly grew louder and more intense. Soon it became a kind of shrill, steady "chirruping" that, while still similar to a bird's song, now seemed strangely more rhythmic and controlled.

———

Dr. Andrew Weincamp heard Moonmare's "chatter" through one of a network of tiny speakers that were part of his HH-OPAL-9 computer control system. The language kept the same pattern and cadence, but in

Weincamp's lab it was generated as a kind of "musical" computerized "tune", recreated from the signals sent from Moonmare back to earth.

Weincamp's pulse raced as again a broad smile appeared on his face. He felt more proud and elated at this moment than any time he could recall in his entire career. But then, this moment was, in a large sense, the culmination of his career.

"Yes..." he whispered, still looking back and forth between the various monitors surrounding him. "Speak to me. God, yes! Tell me all you see!"

Weincamp then quickly activated a new program. With several touches on a nearby monitor face a display appeared titled:

Functions - Intermediate

In the next few moments Moonmare gained her feet.

As she stood, legs apart, teetering slightly in the lunar night, her silhouette against the stars resembled a horse's. The physical resemblance, however, like her chirruping voice, was not exact. She was too large to be a horse. And her body was round and plump. Her legs were too short and thick for a horse, and although her long neck jutted upward against the glistening trails of stars, she appeared to have no mane. And the head at the top of her neck did not seem quite like a horses. As it began to move about, glancing from side to side, it appeared somewhat round and much larger than a horse's. It seemed to also be missing the characteristic pointed ears.

She leaned, contracted her muscles, lifted her huge hooves and edged slightly backward and forward. The first of these small steps were unsteady, but after several attempts they became easier and instinctively more coordinated.

———

Four hours later Weincamp activated still another program. This one was entitled:

Functions - Advanced

Almost immediately Moonmare began moving freely around the remains of the cylindrical craft - strutting, chirruping, making quick starts and stops and sudden turns. As she engaged in this "play", she occasionally stopped, cocked her head, and peered upward into the stars or away at the black spines of mountain ranges and crater rims.

Like all newborn things, Moonmare seemed excited, quizzical, and even eager to get on with the possibilities of her odd new life. With no parent or other living thing present, however, she also seemed to be waiting.

FIVE

Muriel sat, eyes closed and breathing slowly, in a large, overstuffed blue chair. The chair and an adjacent chrome lamp dominated one corner of the office loft of Dr. Cynthia Weil. It faced out from a large sunlit window beside a wall of books.

Cynthia was a thin, homely woman with bright hazel eyes, dense freckles and darkened "granny" glasses perched near the tip of her nose. A huge, frizzy clutch of red hair surrounded her pointed face. At this moment she sat just to the side of Muriel.

Leaning forward, she whispered, "Now, imagine you're getting a little heavier and sinking deeper into the chair every time you let out a breath… Feel that weight? . .and the wonderful sense of stillness and relaxation?"

Muriel nodded slightly.

"Keep the long, slow breaths going," Cynthia continued. "That's the key… Each time you exhale you sink a little deeper."

As Muriel concentrated on the slow, pronounced rhythm of her chest rising and falling, Cynthia watched for nearly a minute. "Good," she said finally. "Remember, this is your own private space. Visualize it... your dark, comfortable and totally secure corner of the universe..."

Muriel remained silent.

"...a place where nothing but calm and tranquility are allowed in. Everything negative has to wait outside... Visualize that. It's all out there... It exists, but it can't get to you here. You're insulated, surrounded by all the cool, wonderful peace you could ever hope for."

After a moment, Muriel smiled slightly and, keeping her eyes closed, said, "Jack?"

Cynthia chuckled. "No, kiddo, not even Jack. This place is yours alone. Save Jack for those Saturday night sessions with a glass of wine in front of the fireplace."

Cynthia and Muriel both smiled. Muriel opened her eyes.

"Good," Cynthia said. "You're feeling what we're after, here, right?"

Muriel nodded.

"You know, hon, I can see you really are getting it. You're starting to realize it's not rocket science. It's like a load that's just gotten too damn heavy and cumbersome to carry around. Now you're teaching yourself how to just put it down and walk away. No magic. No miracles. Just plain old common sense and a few simple techniques."

SIX

Most travelers passing by SAMS, the Saltridge Astronomical Monitoring Station, never realized it was there. Those few who happened to look up at just the right spot off Highway 10 for just the right few seconds, probably regarded what they saw between two distant hills, as a small radar facility built into the side of a rocky ledge.

About fifty miles northwest of the town of Arroyo Alto, California, the installation appeared to consist of three small, Quonset buildings, several radar and microwave towers and a heliport. All of this was surrounded by an area of parched, God-forsaken earth and a tall, chain-link fence crowned with coils of razor wire and warning signs threatening electrical shock on contact. A single lane dirt road lead into the facility and the most activity anyone had ever noticed there - including the two hundred or so residents of nearby Arroyo Alto - was the occasional comings and goings of black, unmarked vehicles and military helicopters. The few private pilots who happened to fly over the area (the facility had been purposely placed outside of any commercial air corridors) were able to get a somewhat better appreciation of the extent of the facility.

Adjacent to the radar towers and buildings in a shallow canyon hidden from the highway, a group of three huge and two smaller dishes were built, like an arrangement of giant woofers and tweeters, into the desert terrain. At their center was a concrete observatory dome housing a large telescope. These structures were spread over nearly ninety acres and were circled and crisscrossed by a single lane, tar roadway. Three small parking lots and seven more Quonset-like buildings also dotted the area.

Only those who knew Saltridge from the inside, however, were aware of its true size and significance. Built on a series of nine, massive, underground floors, the facility housed a full American Space Agency Control Center, a state-of-the-art observatory, an astronomical research wing, and a small National Security Agency contingent. Along with these operations came the administrative offices, housing, recreational and other services and facilities required to keep the complex operating independently, around the clock.

Saltridge was a top secret facility put slowly and quietly into place over an eight year period. Though it was shown in government record books as an astronomical research and development complex, much of its equipment and a specialized, classified group of inhabitants had one mission - to provide full time support for the Moonmare project.

One of those inhabitants, the man who had created Moonmare and who had been closely monitoring the first moments of her "life", was Andrew Weincamp.

Weincamp looked nothing like the genius he was. A world-renowned genetic physicist of fifty-one years might well be imagined as fat, bald and spectacled. Weincamp, however, looked more like a thirty-five year old cover model for an issue of "Gentlemen's Quarterly". His thin, handsome face was framed with a mane of shoulder length, wavy, white-blond hair. His eyes were a calm and steady slate gray. A pair of thin, wire-rimmed glasses added a sense of intelligence to his long, masculine nose and shallow cheeks, and his slender, six foot two inch body was hard and tan.

While an assortment of CRT's, scanners, digital drives, and hard copy printers surrounded him, at this moment Weincamp was intent on a twin computer monitor arrangement built into a wall panel. Above one monitor a brass plate had been engraved with the letters "EM BRN". Above the other were the letters "LOG BRN". On the face of each screen clustered rows of numbers, dots, spaces, and hieroglyphic-type figures appeared in a constantly scrolling stream of digital information. The appearance of these clusters represented the tones and pulses that were the "language" spoken by Moonmare, some two hundred and forty-thousand miles away, on the far side of the moon.

Weincamp and his technical staff had been working with these monitors and many other pieces of state-of-the-art equipment for many months before Moon-mare's lunar "birth". And their diligence had paid off. Everything had gone off precisely as planned. She was doing exactly what Weincamp's calculations had told him she would do.

To cap off the morning, a technician came over the intercom informing Weincamp of a call. It was Vice President, Martin Balk. Balk was in an unmarked government jet, en route to a little known airstrip in the town of Palm Desert. "Drew," he said over the scrambled air phone, "are we a success?"

"It seems so," Weincamp replied.

"What's her status?"

"She's conscious, on her feet, and talking to us. Here, have a listen." Weincamp held the phone up to a nearby speaker that was generating Moonmare's voice tones.

"That's actually her?"

"Yes. And even as an infant, talking with great verbosity about her surroundings."

"Incredible! And the tests?"

"So far all positive and all exactly as we had projected."

"Drew, you're amazing!" Balk said.

Weincamp knew these weren't the typical, political attaboys Balk was so accomplished at handing out. He knew that in this case, the politician's words were sincere. He was truly amazed, delighted and no doubt, very relieved.

"So what's next?" Balk continued.

"We'll need another fifteen hours or so to finish up everything and stabilize her."

"Then?"

"We'll activate Caller 4 and start her on her way."

"And a new era in genetic engineering and geographical space exploration begins. You'd better be damn proud of yourself, Drew!"

Weincamp smiled as the digital figures marched up the screens and the pleasant series of tones continued. "Thanks, Martin," he replied. "I am....very proud."

"Good. Now finish getting her off to wherever it is she's headed, then get yourself some rest - pronto! I'll see you tomorrow morning."

Yes, things looked good, very good. And they continued to look good for the next fifteen hours while all acclimation, coordination and communication functions were being carried out.

Then Weincamp gave the command to activate Caller 4.

SEVEN

Less than thirty seconds after the Caller's activation, a shock of fright rose up through the lunar ground into Moonmare's entire being. She jerked, legs outspread, and froze for an instant of confused horror. Her sudden, high-pitched "screech" then cut off like a needle yanked across a record.

The source of her nightmare resided at a spot seven-hundred and thirty kilometers away. It was at this location, also on the backside of the moon, that Caller 4 stood on the gentle slope of a lunar hillside. The unit looked like a four by four, twelve foot tall ingot of brushed aluminum, standing on end and half-buried in the lunar soil. Surrounding it were the signs of a downward rocket engine blast and behind it, connected to it by a white, telescoping metal arm, was a small, long inactive, unmanned landing craft. Two features were plainly visible on the Caller - the large, embossed, red "4" on its upper face and a twenty-four inch, glass-like square on its lower face, just above the lunar soil. Before activation, the square had been black. But now it had turned a bright, slowly pulsating sky blue. At the same time, the Caller had begun to generate a steady, rhythmic series of vibrations from its internal metallic windings, out into the lunar soil.

Seconds after it began, Moonmare realized exactly what the vibrations meant. It was then that her voice returned. But it was no longer a pleasant rhythmic chirruping. It had become a series of frantic screeches, like fingernails stabbing at a cosmic chalkboard. At the same instant she reared high on her thick hind legs, her huge rump quivering. She tossed her head in the stars. Drool flung out in long, slimy webs from her mouth. Her eyes rolled and bulged. Her hooves dropped back onto the lunar ground with the impact of tremendous boulders and she began to gallop as fast as her short, massive legs would carry her.

Her direction was instinctive and unchangeable - directly toward the distant, vibrating object known as Caller 4.

———

Weincamp had expected her to be startled. He had planned on seeing the pause in the numbers as she became conscious of the realization sent out by the Caller. But her internal functions were then supposed to have intervened. A specific portion of the signal was to have been overridden. She was supposed to have been calmed and the numbers were to return to normal as she moved out across the lunar plain.

Instead, the numbers went crazy.

Weincamp entered an adjustment into the computer and saw no change.

He tried again and still another time.

No change.

He ran a rapid series of program alterations again, with no luck.

Finally, feeling his chest constrict, he barked an order over the intercom to a technician two floors down at the mainframe. "Two brain scan. Immediately."

The technician heard the urgency in the scientist's voice. "Yes, Doctor. Is something —"

"Now!" Weincamp interrupted.

"Yes, Doctor!"

"And do an A.S. on the logical software."

"Yes, Doctor. The 'Emotional', too?"

"Yes. No! No, I'll deal with that myself. Just *hurry,* damn it!"

"Yes, Doctor."

It was at that moment that Weincamp saw something just as frightening as the nonsensical pattern of numbers coming through - something that was rarely, if ever, supposed to happen. A close similarity - a near repetition in the information on the EM BRN screen at very short intervals.

The clusters now appearing were:

01221]-03475 2370-[[756 14040 33325

```
01220]-33475 237-[(-590756 122060[403375-
]47435 658 0106
122-0160[[59166
433477 40H-3324- 658 [[59166
```

Five minutes later Weincamp got to his feet and left the room. In the hallway he passed a guard who noted that he appeared oddly pale and rushing as if nearly panicked.

"Morning, Doctor," the guard said.

Weincamp didn't return the greeting. He was thinking forward thirty minutes to a different computer screen. The trouble was, even before the translations were done, he was afraid he knew what she was trying to say.

———————

When Martin Balk entered Weincamp's private office the next morning he found the doctor seated in the dark, staring past a computer translation screen, into the light of a small lamp.

Balk placed a congratulatory bottle of champagne on a long, metal credenza and moved toward the scientist. He was unable to see the computer screen, but he could see Weincamp's face. It had none of the young, vibrant features of the man he knew. It showed exhaustion, fear, and guilt. Even worse for Balk, it showed failure. He was about to ask Weincamp what was wrong when, without looking up, the doctor spoke. "The logical brain motivation override has failed."

"But can't you—"

"I've tried."

"So what exactly does that mean? What's happening with her? Is she still running?"

"Yes. At full speed."

"Well, that's good. See there. At least—"

"And pleading."

He swiveled the computer screen and Balk looked down.

The digital numeric sequences of Moonmare's speech had been translated into the equivalent of human language. The message was a continuous one, running off the bottom of the screen. Weincamp scrolled it up to the end. Balk saw a repetition of:

Please! Help!
Please!
I can't!
Help! I can't!
Help! Stop!
Please!
Help!

Weincamp looked up at Balk. "We're driving her mad with fear," he said calmly.

EIGHT

Jack and Muriel took a seat on a wooden bench under a huge ornate dome that was the center of the hub display at the recently completed Southwest Flight and Space Museum. Above them, suspended by wires, was a single, massive jet engine from a Saturn V rocket – one of three remaining that had been the first workhorses of the American Lunar Space Program.

People milled around the couple on all sides. Groups and individuals of assorted nationalities passed by checking floor maps, discussing points of interest with their guides, panning palm-sized video cameras, and verifying presentation times on their schedules and brochures.

Surrounding the crowds, on the walls and down each of four corridors that led out from the central hub where Jack and Muriel had sat down, were hundreds of paintings, sculptures, suspended artifacts, historical documents, and other display items that told the complete story of American space flight.

Muriel was frightened.

Minutes before, the couple had been wandering amongst displays as they had done many other times at museums like this. Jack, as always, had been rambling on excitedly about things like the absolute nature of light speed, the relationship of mass to gravity, and the future possibilities of travel to various planets in the solar system.

Muriel had been thinking to herself that no matter how many museum halls they walked, it never ceased to amaze her how the spark would flash in his eyes when the subject turned to flight or space. It was precisely because she had been through many conversations like this that she recognized immediately when something had changed.

In the midst of his predictions on the remaining life of the Voyager 1 spacecraft, Jack paused for just an instant. Something in his manner suddenly changed. The spark still hovered, still bright, but somehow it was different. If asked to, Muriel would not have been able to even guess what had just happened in his mind, but she knew something had, and whatever it was, it was not typical of her Jack.

For the next twenty minutes, as they wandered from one exhibit to another, the subtle changes continued to intensify. He became quieter, more thoughtful and serious, less like a kid surrounded by everything he'd wished for on Christmas morning.

It was when they had reached the center, under the huge domed hub of the museum, that he suddenly sat Muriel down and took her hands in his. He looked into her eyes with dead seriousness and said, "Honey, I have to talk with you."

She took a quick breath and held it in her chest. Her throat began to constrict. His lips parted and she was positive the end of their relationship was at hand. In the split second before he spoke she went over the entire familiar list: How could she have ever thought this wonderful, handsome man would really want to stay with her? How could he still want to make love to her after seeing her uncovered body on an almost weekly basis? How could she have been crazy enough to get carried away with this whole thing? How could a man of such intelligence and stature be attracted to a woman like her? A liar like her? How could she have ever really believed the fairy tale would—

"Muriel," he said quietly, "there's only one way to say this and that's straight out."

She closed her eyes and waited for it - *Sorry, it's been nice but—*

"I love you. In a way I just can't make sense of. Like I've never loved anything or anyone before. It's happened fast, I know, and I'm not even sure how or why, but here we are, and..." He paused for a long moment, then brought out the ring box and opened it. "I want you with me for the rest of my life. Will you marry me?"

She looked down at the ring - a large, glistening diamond, the likes of which she had been positive she would never in her lifetime own. It was this sight, along with Jack's words and all else she had been feeling for this man, that suddenly sent her emotional balance totally out of equilibrium. She heard her voice from a distance as she broke into tears whispering, "Oh, God!"

Then the bright, immense tile floor was moving under her feet. She was darting over it like a panicked sparrow desperate to find a door or window – an escape. People turned, staring as she rushed by, wondering if she'd been hurt. Then, in a moment, a glass door swung wide and she found the sunlight, a flash of leaves and flowers and finally two fountains. She ended up kneeling in the grass between a statue and a hedge.

Jack was with her immediately. He knelt and held her arms, saying, "Sweetheart, calm down! It's okay! If you need some time I understand!"

Then her voice was back inside her body and she felt it was pent up with a hundred times the excitement Jack felt when he saw a rocket or played with a computer or talked about the speed of light. Before she knew how or why, all of her emotions just welled up and poured out. "Too soon? Are you out of your spaced-out mind, Jack Moore? Too *soon*? You *idiot*! I'll marry right *now*, this *second*! This *instant*! God, I love you so much! Oh, my God!" She threw her arms around him and began to cry.

After he had calmed her down they found an isolated bench beside a stone walkway. Jack told Muriel he had spent hours thinking about the past few months and he now felt he should be absolutely clear about what he wanted for their future. "I know it's only been about six months now," he said, "but it's been an incredible six months and you came into my life at a time when some important decisions had to be made anyway... decisions like my retirement from the astronaut program and the Air Force."

"What? But, Jack, you love the Air Force!"

"Please, just listen. It's *you* I love. You're the first *real* thing that's happened to me in years, and I can't let that reality pass me by."

"But, Jack, your whole life has been about space and airplanes and all those things! Why give all that up? You don't have to! We can still get married."

"Sweetheart, I'm over fifty now, and the reality is I'll probably never get to space. I'll most likely spend the rest of my Air Force career behind a desk. I want something *real* to look forward to now. I want to accomplish real things. Family things. I want a house and kids and a basketball net in the driveway, and a swing set. Somehow you woke all that up in me. It may sound corny, but I feel like my clock is ticking, and I can't let it run out. I've realized *you're* what I've been waiting for all along, and you're what I want to dedicate my life to."

"Jack, are you sure?"

"I got an offer from an old, retired buddy of mine. He's flying now for a large airline company. I'd have to start with freight, but I can go to work with him any time and we don't even have to move! Okay?"

Before the tears overcame her again she found enough composure to say, "Whatever you want is what I want! Of course it's okay!"

Then they were in each other's arms again. The dream had come true after all. Amazing as it seemed, he loved her as she'd always hoped. He was hers and everything was right.

Almost everything...

NINE

At fifteen minutes after nine a.m., five months and seven days after the birth of Moonmare, Andrew Weincamp walked into the men's room on Level Three, Wing J, at Saltridge.

Weincamp had always been a thin man, but these days he looked emaciated. Substantial weight loss, however, was only one manifestation of the changes the scientist had been going through. He was also pale. His tanned, smooth skin had become leathery and sallow. He was unshaven today, as was often the case recently, and his long blond hair, once like a heavy, silky mane, was now much shorter, straw-like and matted. The scientist's rumpled brown slacks and corduroy jacket put the final touches on his unkempt image.

This, in fact, was Weincamp's own assessment as he stepped up to the brown marble sink top, bent over in front of one of the faucets and soaked his hung-over face with several handfuls of water. A moment later he removed a paper towel from the dispenser and began to dry himself.

Suddenly the door swung open and Martin Balk walked in. Balk looked at his watch. "Well, twenty-five minutes late this time," he snapped. "A new record, Drew. Drinking even more these days?"

Weincamp didn't bother to acknowledge. He was too tired and felt too bad. Balk, however, wasn't content to let it drop. "Of course, in your estimation I guess leaving four of the most important men in the United States twiddling their thumbs is probably appropriate behavior. You seem to be proving time and again, Drew, that you just don't give a damn."

"I'm sorry," Weincamp whispered.

"Oh, I see. You're sorry again. If my memory serves me right, that makes three apologies this month alone. So I should just start —"

"Martin, please!"

Balk took a deep breath. He turned around, stepped quickly to the opposite wall and urinated. He returned to the sink and began washing his hands. During this time Weincamp had leaned forward, placing his large hands on the marble counter top. He kept peering into the mirror as if carefully inspecting each tiny, new wrinkle on his face.

Finally Balk spoke again. "So, have you decided?" he asked. Weincamp gave no response.

"She's suffering, Drew," Balk said. And now the tone in his voice had changed. The anger and disgust had disappeared. Suddenly he had become Weincamp's good old friend and compassionate advisor. "She's running around up there, useless and out of her mind, Drew. She's suffering. And now this growth problem. I'm sorry it's taken me this time to realize it, but it's true. You know that. You're the one who first said so."

Again Balk waited for a response, but Weincamp didn't move or speak. "Is that what you want, now?" Balk continued. "Suddenly you've changed and decided to just abandon her?"

The scientist lowered his face, looked down into the sink, and slowly shook his head. Balk placed his hand on Weincamp's back. He leaned down close to the scientist and whispered, "Then help me do something about it! Give me your support in this. You're the key, Drew. You're her creator. They'll follow your lead! If you give the word we can put her out of her misery, and that's what she needs now. She needs peace!"

Weincamp straightened up. He turned and faced the politician. "Martin," he said, "I have been trying for five of the longest months of my life to convince you to give her peace. You wouldn't hear of it. You have insisted time and again that she is a non-living, unfeeling thing – a 'meat machine'. You have degraded my work, embarrassed me in front of my staff, and made it clear that you felt if we let her wander around up there long enough while we tried one software change after another, perhaps some shred of return would eventually come from her. Now, suddenly, things have changed. Now you've regained whatever infinitesimal bit of compassion for her you might have once had. Why is that, my friend? Because now she's become a fly in the soup of your political future? Because now there is actually a possibility the public may find out that presidential candidate Martin Balk backed the creation of a living mutation?"

"She's not a—"

"But she is! She's *alive*, damn it, and you know that!"

"She is not a living organism by scientific standards!" Weincamp slammed his palm down on the counter. "You've known all along that she has emotions, fears, a conscious awareness! You've seen those horrific translations. You've heard her screeching and pleading. Did you think those godforsaken pleas came out of nowhere? Did you think I invented them? Did you really think a machine, a 'meat machine' as you so tactlessly put it, could feel those things?"

Balk clenched his teeth and took another deep breath. Though it was difficult, he remained in form. He knew that was critical now. He sensed that Weincamp was on the verge of a mental collapse. This meant he might also be on the verge of talking to the world, and Balk couldn't allow that to happen. He had to keep this man quiet and on his side for at least a short time longer. "I only know that she's out of control and her life needs to be ended — and it has to happen fast. And I know I need your help to convince the members of this committee."

Weincamp, too, took a deep breath. "Relax," he said. "You'll get my support. I don't want to see her running around up there out of her mind anymore than you do."

As he said this Weincamp saw Balk's face change. With these few words the Vice President's fears were swept away. In his mind the probability of Moonmare disappearing, without so much as a trace, had just become an excellent one.

The scientist wasn't finished, however. "But there's one thing I demand," he said.

"And that is?"

"I want samples. Both brains, tissue, bones, and various organs. It's only with those in hand that I can hope to tell what happened with this growth cycle reaction, and maybe correct some of the horrible injustice we've both been involved in."

"But, Drew, that means—"

"I know what it means and I know you owe it to me. When you decided on this presidential run, you abandoned me, Martin. You walked out of the lab and onto the TV screens like none of it had ever existed. And like the dutiful silent partner, I've kept my mouth shut for months now, watching what I created turn into a nightmare. But the fact is, you're not only a party to this nightmare, but a co-creator. You set up those screenings. It was your people and your money. You spent American taxpayer dollars, Martin – one hell of a lot of them – to help create a monster."

"Drew, please. It's not in our—"

"And we both know that if the public finds out what you've done, not only your presidential candidacy but your career as a public servant isn't worth the crap you're made of. In fact, you and I might both end up in jail. Personally, I'm at a point in my life where I really don't care much about that."

"But this is highly classified information."

"I could give a shit less. The only thing that matters to me now is trying to right at least some of the wrong I've done. How about you? What matters to you, Martin? Your freedom? Moonmare? The presidency?"

Balk knew the scientist was right. It had all been a calculated risk, a kind of systematic, career crap shoot. Had the Moonmare project been a success he would now be the man who'd had the foresight and wisdom to lead the United States into the stars. There still would have been the need for cover ups, of course – tissue acquisitions mainly, and the fact that she probably really did have a kind of consciousness – but all that could have been accomplished – if she had just been a success and Weincamp hadn't started off the deep end.

As it was, however, if word got out, Balk knew he would be political rump roast in the public meat grinder. Not only would Moonmare be considered a gross misuse of federal dollars, he would be viewed as a governmental Frankenstein – a kind of mad, inhumane political mind who had secretly tampered with the stuff of life. He also knew that although they could kill her from afar, the best way to thoroughly "clean up" Moonmare's demise, and be sure her existence had been completely erased, was with a manned mission. "Okay," he said. "I think I can convince them to go back up there. But other than your samples we eliminate all traces of her."

"Fine. As humanely as possible."

"Probably a nuke."

Weincamp looked up at the vice president. "I can't imagine any other way to guarantee a complete job."

For the first time during this meeting a slight smile crossed Andrew Weincamp's face. It was not a pleasant or friendly smile, however, and Balk could see that. It was a smile that was motivated partly by satisfaction and partly by pity. "Ah, the obsession with power," Weincamp said, smiling and shaking his head. "The awesome grip…"

Balk was unmoved. "You get the samples, I get the Presidency, and the public is none the wiser… Agreed?"

Weincamp had come to hate Balk with a passion he could not quite define. But he, too, had little choice and he knew it. "Agreed," he said.

———

Two hours later a decision was made between six men in a small conference room. Following that decision Martin Balk stood up at the head of a large oak table and made a statement:

"Gentlemen, having your complete agreement on this matter, let me summarize. As quickly as can be arranged, a three person team will embark on a top secret moon landing.

"An area previously constructed and dedicated for observation purposes will be utilized as a base. Moonmare will be called to that location and destroyed using a series of explosive charges and umbilical shut down.

"Following her demise, a series of flesh samples will be acquired from Moonmare as determined by Doctor Weincamp. After acquisition of the samples, our landing team will leave the moon's surface and enter a temporary orbit. During this time a precisely positioned nuclear charge will be detonated at the site.

"All trace of Moonmare will be erased. Any inquiries from other countries that may become aware of the nuclear event will be answered with assumptions made out of our 'ignorance'. Our position will be that we assume a meteor impact on the backside of the moon, but have no proof or confirmation of any kind.

"The Moonmare team will be disbanded and all details of this mission and the Moonmare project in its entirety will remain at the highest levels of secrecy, indefinitely."

Following the statement Balk paused, then glanced around the table and said, "Agreed?"

One by one the men nodded their heads, answering in the affirmative.

TEN

Nine hours later Martin Balk had flown back to Washington, attended a short budget meeting, and taken care of several important administrative issues.

With these things accomplished he left Capital Hill via helicopter for his private home in the Maryland countryside. Once there, he immediately called his wife and told her he was up to his ears in important matters and would be spending the night taking care of them.

Calls like this were a frequent occurrence for Adrianne Balk. On many occasions she accompanied Martin when he went into "hiding" in the country to catch up on his paperwork. But on this night he didn't ask, and she wasn't in the mood anyway. Instead, she simply wished her husband well, reminded him to take his allergy medication, and returned to her reruns of "CSI New York".

Ten minutes later Martin Balk sat outside in tennis shorts and a T-shirt on a large redwood deck. While sipping a double scotch, he languished in the balmy spring air, glancing from constellation to constellation picking out familiar stars. He also pondered the opportunities the day's events had laid before him.

Balk always tried to think in terms of opportunities. He considered positive thinking the most likely way to succeed when approaching any problem or situation. There were always beneficial results to be had. The trick, in certain cases, was to figure out just what they might be. And that is exactly what he had been doing for the past hour. In this case, he had decided the opportunities were substantial. First, as a result of the day's meeting, he would be allowed to continue his climb to the presidency unencumbered. Second, the mechanics had finally been put in place to resolve a situation which had been an irritation and a burden to him for months now — the Moonmare failure. Third, and this one he decided on just as his eyes found the small, glittering, irregular cluster of stars known as Pleiades, he would soon be rid of another constant irritation in his life. And that would lead to very productive times he was sure.

"Yes," he whispered out loud. "Opportunities." Then he took another sip of the scotch and picked up the telephone.

He dialed a number and waited. After several rings the line was answered by a female voice. "Hello," the woman said with a tone of quiet indifference.

"Hello, there," Balk responded, jovially.

The woman was silent. Balk continued, "Wonderful evening, isn't it?"

"Yes."

"You know, I'm sitting here under a sky full of stars, realizing just how incredibly full of opportunities life really is."

The woman said nothing. Balk chuckled. "Of course, you wouldn't know it by the happenings out west right now. I just got in from California. Problems out there."

The woman seemed only slightly curious. "I see. Anything we can help with?"

"Yes, actually it's something appropriate for your group."

"L.A.?"

"Close. The high desert."

"I see."

"I'll follow with instructions tomorrow," he said.

"Fine. By courier?"

"Exactly."

"We look forward to receiving it."

"Good." Balk smiled and hung up the phone. He relaxed into the deep, soft suede of his lounge chair. "Yes," he said out loud again, "wonderful, wonderful opportunities."

ELEVEN

When Jack Moore clicked on "Secure Mail", a front view of a red, rural mailbox appeared on his computer screen. Beneath it was a request for two passwords. He entered them and an instant later the computer beeped and the door of the mailbox flipped down. The image then appeared to move forward until the blackness inside the box filled the screen. When it stopped an icon of the planet Saturn appeared. Beneath it were the letters "ASNAi".

Jack double clicked on the icon. Another password. The computer started through a series of half-muted hums and beeps. At the same time, the mailbox moved back in and rotated to a side view. Its flag swiveled up into a vertical position and on the flag was another icon – a tiny American Flag with a key in front of it.

Jack clicked on the flag and key while at the same time holding down the "Control–Home +" keys. Immediately a short phrase appeared in the center of the screen.

"Accessing: Buffer Code Alpha, Please."

Jack typed in another code – the name "iMuriel".

"Enter Buffer Code Loop."

Jack typed in: "101040040101"

The computer immediately displayed new text telling Jack it was checking his security buffer. A few moments later the following message appeared:

(1) Correspondence Received

>   Read
>   File
>   Delete
>   Escape

Jack clicked on "Read".

The screen changed again. It was still the side view of the mailbox, but now an envelope floated out of its opening and levitated toward Jack on the screen. In a moment it had covered the mail box. On its face was the heading:

Jack Moore: ASNA Security Mail – 101040040101

A white page lifted up out of the envelope, unfolded and came full center screen. In addition to the time and date, it read:

To: Lt. Colonel Jack Moore -

From: Regular Guy Jack Moore (World Famous Computer Whiz)

Subject: E-Mail Test – New Security Buffer Access

Text:
Dear Lt. Colonel Jack Moore,
This happens to be your first ASNAi secure message. You are writing this message to yourself (you handsome devil, you) in order to test your new ASNAi security e-mail descrambler software package and high speed, digital modem. If you receive this e-mail (sent, incidentally, from Muriel's lap top) you can rest assured that your computer, your program and your secret buffer are working correctly. And you have succeeded once again in completing a highly professional software installation. May the force be with you.
Sincerely,
Regular Guy Jack Moore

Jack whispered, "Perfect."

Callisto, Jack's four month old Airedale puppy, heard the whisper. He had been dozing in a wash of warm sunlight in his usual spot on the carpet by the sliding glass door. He lifted his rust colored head off his paws and perked up both triangular, floppy ears. Jack saw the pup's movement out of the corner of his eye. "Relax, Cal," he said with a smile. "No dog mail."

Callisto seemed to understand. He dropped his head back onto his paws and sighed. The black and rust colored, tightly kinked hair that covered his body glistened in the bright dusty sunlight. He stretched, yawned, and rolled onto his side.

Just as Jack was about to file his letter in what his software called "The Drawer", he heard a movement behind him and saw the reflection of an image appear on the monitor screen.

It was Muriel, just out of the shower. She had stepped up behind him with a towel wrapped around her.

Jack swiveled around in his chair. "Wow," he said.

Muriel leaned forward and gave him a quick kiss on the lips. "Neat program?" she asked, squelching the romantic moment.

"Amazing," Jack replied with that familiar 'new computer toy' ring of excitement in his voice. "Technically I'm not supposed to have it installed off the base but, hey, I gotta have at least one or two perks for all the crap I put up with. Here, I'll show you."

He swiveled back around in his chair and began keying in information. He returned the program to the main menu and took Muriel through the access sequence.

"Looks pretty hush-hush to me," she said.

"Exactly. But since you're soon to be my wife, I can trust you, right?"

Muriel smiled and cocked her head.

"I figured. By the way, my secret buffer code and loop, as long as you keep hanging around wrapped in wet towels, that is, happens to be based on…"

Muriel watched as the screen changed to an array of small, rectangular, gray boxes in which were the basic passwords, control values and parameters of the e-mail program. In the box beneath the words "Buffer Code" was her name. In another was the numeric loop code. Jack then went into Explorer and navigated to a folder titled "iMuriel". "Another 'No-No'. But since I forget a lot these days, and I doubt any terrorists will be breaking in any time soon, I keep them all handy in this folder."

"You know," she said with a coy smile, "I'm beginning to think you really do plan to marry me."

At that moment, she glanced to her left and noticed Cal. "Think Cal will give his blessings?" They both turned. The dog was still lying on his side enjoying the warmth of his sunbath. His eyes had rolled back into half dreaming slits.

Jack and Muriel both chuckled. Muriel turned and started out of the room. As she walked away she said, "You get yourself off that computer, officer Moore, and into some clothes. We've got an appointment at Anna's Invitations in forty minutes flat."

Jack looked down at his watch. She was right. He had gotten carried away again. He filed the letter, made his way back to the main menu, and exited the program.

He got to his feet and crossed the room to Callisto. He knelt and took a moment to stroke the puppy. "You? Not accept her?" he said. "My pal Cal? Never happen." He gave the dog a final pat on the tummy, got to his feet and headed for the master bedroom.

When he stepped in he found Muriel standing in her panties and bra in front of the bathroom mirror, staring at herself. The levity had passed. She looked depressed. Jack knew at once this meant trouble. In the six months he'd come to know Muriel, he'd realized that her self-esteem was virtually non-existent. She suffered deep feelings of inferiority and a paralyzing fear of being alone. Though Jack didn't like these faults, he'd also discovered that Muriel had other traits he found deeply attractive. Her intelligence and shyness had drawn him immediately. He had also come to love her vulnerability and the depths to which she seemed to need and depend on him. He felt he'd become a pillar of stability in her life and he found that knowledge greatly rewarding. On top of all this, from the first time they had made love, he'd found her sexually magnetic. During the months they had come to know and care for each other he had accepted both the positive and negative aspects of this woman as different facets of a complex and extremely sensitive individual – one he'd grown increasingly attached to.

In their first few months, as her negative issues had surfaced, he hadn't questioned her about them. He'd decided that would come in time if their relationship continued to develop. Then, one evening she'd finally come clean. It had been a teary and difficult conversation after a fireside dinner and several glasses of wine. Though she hadn't elaborated, she told Jack her problems stemmed from an abusive childhood. She'd been the only child of a physically violent mother and a basically absent, alcoholic father — both of whom had since died.

Standing behind her now, Jack wondered just how traumatic life must have been for her. He was imagining the kinds of abuses she must have gone through when she turned from the mirror to speak.

"Before you say a word," Jack interrupted, "listen to me. You are more sexually attractive to me right at this moment than you can possibly understand. And if you make one — hear me now — even one of your typically insecure, neurotic statements, I'll feel obligated to console you, which in turn will mean making love to you on the spot – Anna's be damned!"

As always, Muriel thought, he'd come through. She had no choice but to laugh. Then, as she removed her bra, in the sexiest voice she could muster, she replied, "What Lieutenant Colonel in his right mind could be attracted to...a body like this?"

Jack shook his head and smiled. He pulled his "T" shirt over his head. "See," he said, "I knew you couldn't do it!"

When they had finished making love she became quiet. "Seems like every time we do this lately," Jack said, "you end up depressed. Not particularly uplifting to the male ego."

She pulled closer to him under the covers. "I'm sorry, honey," she said. "I just have to keep telling myself, 'Muriel, this is really true. This man wants to marry you. He really does! Love is for the not so beautiful, too.'"

"How many times do I have to tell you, damn it, you *are* beautiful! And that beauty is on top of all the other things about you that *really* matter."

"Jack, I'm–"

"And quit saying you're sorry!" Jack sat up on the bed. "You've been seeing this psychologist for how long now — five months?"

"Yes."

"Well, what has she done for you? Are you feeling better about yourself?"

"Yes," Muriel said, somewhat unconvincingly, "I am. It's taking time but things *are* better."

"Sometimes I wonder if all the crap you had to put up with as a kid was—"

Muriel placed her hand over his mouth. "Shhh," she said, and now there were tears in her eyes. "Honey, I'm almost there. Really. I just feel lucky to have you, that's all. And my confidence is getting better every day you're a part of my life. I promise. I just need you to promise *me* you'll always be here, and be patient with me."

In Moonmare's world the dark expanse was not a place or a thing separate from her body. It was a part of her — not the dense, ungainly part, but a much less cumbersome thing. A thing that was colder or hotter at different times. It was also still and languid, although a part of her was moving. And it was somehow divided, though it had no clearly defined borders or segments.

One part of the darkness, the most dominant in her consciousness, was a kind of partial, horrible recognition. Had she had true awareness and a human vocabulary she would have called this recognition "sheer panic" or "fright". Without intelligence, however, those two words did not exist for her. What she sensed, therefore, became more like a very simple awareness of how those things felt. The feeling was something like the split second realization on the part of a man who has just passed the point of no return in an accidental fall from a ten story build-

ing — the sudden, excruciating knowledge that, as the street below shot upward, all existence was about to end.

She had no question of why this was the case in part of her darkness, nor could she have placed it or assigned a weight or percentage to it. It was just there, and unlike the realization of the falling man, her panic did not end a few seconds later at the moment of impact. It was constant and unyielding — a seemingly eternal stream of horror going on and on as an inherent part of her existence.

Another part of her darkness was something like a need. This, too, existed as only a partial awareness in her mind. She simply sensed that something was missing — something important that she wanted very badly.

There were other undefined parts of her darkness. One was the equivalent of a great, long weariness and a sense of being continually pulled downward. Another was a simple, very primitive conviction that somewhere out in the farthest reaches of her being, somewhere incredibly distant, there was an answer, an escape, a tiny, almost non-existent shred of hope.

This was the smallest part of her existence.

But it was also the part that kept her running.

TWELVE

Several days after his meeting with Martin Balk and the other members of the Moonmare council, Andrew Weincamp left his home just after sunset and drove to Saint Angelica's Catholic Church in the nearby town of Twenty-Nine Palms.

Saint Angelica's was a small church in a run-down, mostly Indian and Mexican neighborhood. Weincamp had discovered it several months earlier while driving aimlessly one night trying to find some release from the guilt he carried inside. On that night he had rounded a corner and seen lights under the pointed arch of the church's opened front doors. That had been on a cool evening in March, and the glow had seemed warm and inviting under the shadowed figures of surrounding pepper and tamarisk trees.

Without giving his actions much thought, he had simply parked his car on the crumbling pavement across the street and walked in. He'd been surprised to find the worn, polished rows of pews completely empty. Not surprising, however, was the peaceful sense of calm that hovered quietly within the ornate walls. Although the rows of stained glass windows were small, and the brightly painted "Stations of the Cross" and cracking cement arches were hardly world class art or architecture, Weincamp found a beauty and serenity in them that was profound.

The crucifix, a ten foot bronze cast of Jesus on a huge, dark wooden cross, stood over the alter and dominated the front of the church. Beneath it, the gold candle holders, the podium, and the abundance of colorful silk and filigreed metal work placed the final delicate touches on Saint Angelica's spiritual beauty.

On that first visit Weincamp hadn't been quite sure of what to do as he entered the church. On this evening, however, he dipped his fingers in the holy water, genuflected and made the sign of the cross. He then moved up the center isle. As he did so he thought that perhaps it was the knowledge that the church's doors were always open that gave him such a sense of peace and tranquility. There was something deeply comforting for him just knowing he could come to this place any time of the day or night.

Whatever the attraction, the scientist had returned several times over the months, and tonight he had come for a special occasion. He had decided to confess. He was not a Catholic by birth, or even a religious person, so when the idea of confession first occurred to him it seemed strange and even somewhat frightening. But the more he'd thought about it, the more he began to feel it was the right thing to do. Eventually he'd come to the conclusion it was a necessity. The act of confessing to a holy man had been the driving force, along with the knowledge that a priest, with his sworn vows of secrecy, was really the only person he could comfortably share his highly classified information with.

He had pondered the idea of when to confess for some weeks. After his last meeting with Balk at Saltridge he had decided to go through with it immediately. Once he had made the decision to tell his story he'd felt enormously relieved. He'd gone on-line, charged with excitement about the prospect of forgiveness, and read up on every detail he could find about the act of confessing in the Catholic Church — the proper words and gestures, the holy water on the forehead, and the communion the next day. He had also learned about the tradition of the rosary and penance — the price he would pay in prayers for his sins.

On this night the church was completely empty except for the priest who would do the confessions. He knelt in black robes at a small individual pew on the right side of the alter. Deep in prayer beneath the crucifix, his forehead rested on his clasped thumbs.

As Weincamp moved up the aisle he first noticed the priest then the open confessional doors to the right. He found a pew near the doors, made the sign of the cross, and knelt.

He gazed up at the crucifix and thought of Moonmare. What was life really like for her? How did she feel? Could her state even be considered life? Was she really as aware of her plight as all the translations had suggested? Or was it, as Balk had always insisted, a numeric, superimposed consciousness — a kind of programmed, high-tech delivery of the data responses appropriate for the situation she was going through. Had he created a being that was *really* suffering so horribly, or was hers just the technical appearance of suffering?

Odd, the scientist thought, that he was supposed to be the brilliant one and he wasn't sure of anything anymore. Then he realized that wasn't true. There was one thing he was positive of. It was the human factor that had made the difference — the tissue. Had the Mare been strictly a synthetic creation, the scientist felt he would now be able to live with what he had done. But she was not. And that was a responsibility no one but he could bear.

The priest made the sign of the cross and got to his feet. He paused for what seemed like a long time, seemingly transfixed beneath the figure of Jesus, then he turned and moved toward the confessional.

At that moment there was a distant noise. It was a sound that Weincamp heard, but only in the back of his mind. A car door had closed out on the street. Moments later, as the priest moved down the alter steps toward the side aisle, there was a second, nearly identical sound. Another door had closed on the same car. Weincamp was so intent on the priest's approach to the confessional door and what he was about to do, that neither sound registered. Instead, he took a deep breath and said, in his mind, "Bless me Father for I have sinned," as he prepared to get to his feet.

The sounds had been made by two people, who, like the doctor, were not local residents. One was a squat, chubby woman in her early fifties. The other was a tall, much younger man, who could have been her son. Though not familiar faces in the area, the two appeared to be the type of people who might live there. Both were dressed modestly, the woman in a muumuu made of bright, flowered material. A light, knitted shawl was wrapped around her shoulders and she had tied a bright pink scarf over her head. The man was dressed in a faded pair of Levis. He wore white tennis shoes, a cluster of keys on his belt, and a Led Zeppelin sweatshirt with the sleeves cut off. As the pair moved away from their car and paused at the front steps of the church, they glanced around casually and saw no movement in the area. This pleased the woman. She nodded with a slight smile and the two started up the steps of Saint Angelica's.

Inside the church, Weincamp had watched the priest enter the confessional and he was now moving toward the door next to the one the priest had entered. When he reached it he noticed his hand was shaking as he pulled on the handle. He entered and closed it behind him. As he did so a small red light on the outside wall above the door came on. This informed other possible confessors the tiny room was in use.

Inside, the room was nearly pitch black and much like a coat closet, Weincamp thought. Above his head was a single, extremely dim light source of some kind. He could only make out a short padded ledge on which to kneel, a wooden counter on which to rest his arms, and a small, connecting screened-off opening between his "closet" and the priest's. The scientist's heart was racing as he knelt on the padded ledge and clasped his hands. He knew he could simply get to his feet and walk back out, and he was seriously considering doing just that, when a panel on the small wooden opening suddenly slid open.

He could hear the priest's voice, whispering prayers in Latin. Through the black screen that now separated the two, Weincamp could only make out the holy man's dim profile. He saw what looked like shadowy hand movements, as if the priest were making the sign of the cross several times in a row. And somehow, when he realized that he had passed the point of no return with his decision, the fright began to leave Weincamp. The breath eased back into his lungs. The vice-like grip of his clasped hands relaxed, and a deep sense of calm settled in his mind. The words, "Bless me Father for I have sinned..." drifted quietly from his lips. The priest continued to whisper his prayers. He was asking God for forgiveness for the scientist. Weincamp knew he had done the right thing.

Meanwhile the "mother" and "son" couple entered the church and dipped their fingers into the holy water. They each made the sign of the cross and genuflected. As they did so, they noticed the red lights on above the confessional doors. They took a moment to glance around the church and were pleased to find it empty. They moved toward the confessional. As they walked, the man handed the woman a pair of thin, white gloves. "Completely empty, here?" he questioned.

"Looks like it," the woman responded, slipping the gloves on.

"Not many sinners in this town."

The woman's face beamed. She smiled the chubby, shiny- cheeked smile of a loving grandmother. Then she straightened the scarf on her head and said, "We better get busy. This can't last, and I need a drink — bad."

Glancing at the lights above the confessionals the man responded, "He'll be on the right?"

"Yup."

As they moved toward the confessional, the man reached into his pocket and slipped on his own pair of gloves. The woman's gloved hand dropped into her purse and found the grip of the twenty-two caliber, semi-automatic pistol, stolen half an hour earlier from a dresser drawer in Weincamp's house.

Meanwhile, Weincamp had begun telling his story. He had expected some reaction from the priest when he said this was his first confession, but there had been none — just the dim hand gestures and more whispered prayers. He told the priest that many years earlier he had, with the help of a prominent political figure, arranged for the theft of several aborted fetus. He said he had discovered, through top secret government research and screening, that the mothers' genetic make-ups were exactly what he required for an experiment he was involved in. Fetal brain and placental stem cells, he stated, were the perfect form in which to acquire those genes. He told the priest that with DNA from the cells he had created his own form of life for the use of the United States Government. He said his creation had become a mutation that was about to be destroyed. He admitted that because of what he had done, his own life had become a nightmare, filled with horrible guilt and shame, and that he needed God's forgiveness.

When he had completed his confession, an unbearable weight had been lifted from Weincamp's soul and he finally felt at peace. The priest had begun dictating his penance when both Weincamp's and the priest's doors were suddenly yanked open at the same instant.

What then transpired took approximately three seconds.

The woman stepped into Weincamp's confessional bent over as if trying to find something on the floor. And for a split second, that's exactly what the scientist thought was happening. An old woman, *a crazy old woman?*, had lost something. She had dropped her rosary or an earring, and for some strange reason she thought it was in his confessional. Following this thought, however, there was a flash of doubt, an instantaneous sinking feeling in his stomach when he heard her husky voice say, "Sorry. Excuse me."

He realized, with those words, that something was terribly wrong. There was a subtle, underlying impatience and callousness attached to the voice that seemed to suggest: *These are not the words of a chubby, sweet Twenty Nine Palms mother. These are the words of a vicious killer.* But it happened so fast, and so effortlessly, there was no time to react.

She stood up and tilted her head, with a sweet, cherubic little smile on her face. She grasped the hair on the top of Weincamp's head, pulled his face back and said, "Here we go. Open wide, now," as if to feed him a spoonful of soup or medicine. Oddly enough he did not resist. Then he felt the hard, cold feel of metal as the tip of the barrel touched the roof of his mouth, and, for Weincamp alone, the first instant of the sound of the blast.

Meanwhile, the priest had been confronted by the man. Like Weincamp, he thought there had simply been a mistake. Then he heard the woman's voice and he, too, immediately sensed evil and grave danger. But just as with the scientist, there was simply no time. The body of a man was upon him. A pair of large hands began to shove his head forward, against the screen. As this was happening, he heard that absurd, somehow evil statement, "Open wide, now". This was followed immediately by a flash and a deafening blast. The next thing the priest saw was a glint on the front edge of a gun barrel through the screen separator. It was then he knew he was about to die. He looked up in the last instant and was able to see the old woman's face in the adjacent "closet". She was smiling, a cheerful sparkle in her tiny blue eyes, as she said, "So long, old fuck."

Then she pulled the trigger.

Following the two shots the pair acted quickly and professionally. The woman immediately removed the clip from the gun, cocked back the slide and pulled out the single bullet left in the chamber. She then released the slide forward. She immediately wrapped the gun into Weincamp's limp hand, placed his finger on the trigger and squeezed it twice. Next, she cocked the slide back again, placed the single bullet back into the chamber and again released the slide forward. She reinserted the clip and let the gun fall, wrapped in the scientists hand, to his side. As she did this her male partner let the priest fall from his stool into the corner. He stepped from the confessional, closed the door, and checked out his sweatshirt. There was blood spray on his side under his left arm. "Shit," he said, and quickly glanced around the church. It was still empty. The woman stepped out, closed the door to Weincamp's side and smiled. The pair headed for the door, each removing their gloves. As they went, the man said, "How about Madison's? I've been dying for some of that caramel corn and nut mix they put out on the bar."

"Caramel corn, my ass," the woman said. "I'm ready for a steak." They reached the front door. The woman placed her fingers in the holy water bowl, touched them to her forehead and said, "On second thought, how about Mexican? Pablo's Terrace has incredible burritos."

"They make me fart," the man said as he used a splash of holy water to wipe the blood from his sweatshirt.

The woman shook her head. "Madison's it is."

THIRTEEN

Several days later, Martin Balk stepped out in front of the small group of mourners beside the grave of Andrew Weincamp. He paused briefly, then spoke. "Andrew Weincamp was a personal friend of mine. He was a brilliant man who will be missed terribly. I worked closely with Andrew over nearly a twenty-year period, and I was one of many people who had enormous respect for him, both as a scientist and a friend. Though much of his work has gone without fanfare or public notice, those of us who were close to him know that Andrew has literally changed the course of genetic research.

"In a strictly professional sense, many of you know that the majority of Weincamp's work focused on the science of genetic engineering. In a much broader, more human sense, his dream was to help give man the ability to explore and eventually colonize the farthest and most hostile regions of space. When we consider his accomplishments, we begin to see that in the field of genetic applications in deep space, Andrew Weincamp opened an amazing door to the universe for us. Had he lived, he might be leading us through that door in the very near future. As it turns out, the door is left ajar and we are now able to peer through it. And while we see incredible opportunities beyond its threshold, we also see tremendous challenges and dangers. We owe it to this great man to face those dangers, to meet those challenges head on and to continue on the path he has set out for us. Thank you."

When the ceremony had concluded, the group began to disperse. Balk walked with another man some distance from the grave and stopped under a towering oak tree, near his limo. He lit a cigarette and spoke to CIA Director, Mason Gillian, one of the group of men who had approved the Moonmare mission.

"Any change in plans?" Gillian asked.

Balk took a long draw off the Winston Light. "I considered it," he said, "but the more I think about it, the more I'm convinced we should go ahead. We might as well cauterize this thing completely."

"And the tissue samples?"

"We'll see. As of now, no change. By the way, we may need some updates in the redundant control room at SAMS. Is it fully functional?"

"Yes."

"Good."

The director nodded and stepped away. Balk entered his limo.

FOURTEEN

Two weeks after the murder of Andrew Weincamp, Jack Moore's doorbell rang at nine A.M. on a Saturday morning.

Jack had just showered and dressed. He'd made himself a cup of decaf and was killing time taking notes from a new computer manual. He was to meet Muriel at ten-thirty at the Canyon City Mall after her weekly therapy session. The two had planned an early brunch, a look through the astronomy section of the mall's bookstore for Jack, and an afternoon of preliminary wedding decisions.

When Jack answered the door he found a young, handsome man, apparently in his late-twenties, standing on his porch. The "kid", as Jack immediately thought of him, had long blond hair and a tanned, roundish face. He was dressed in cargo shorts and a surfer's T-shirt. Jack expected to hear the youngster say something like,

"Hi, I'm, like, your new paperboy, dude," or "Mister, can I please wash your car for five bucks?".

Instead the "kid" produced a wallet in which was an American Space National Administration identification card. Sure enough, his picture was on it, and his name and title was shown as Darrell Coenan, Personnel Specialist. By the birth date shown, Jack quickly calculated he was thirty-one years old – at least five years older than he looked.

"Lieutenant Colonel Moore?" he asked with a sparkle in his clear brown eyes.

"Yes."

The kid smiled. "Hi," he said, "I'm Darrell Coenan, from the ASNA." He folded his wallet and continued. "I've got an important request for you, sir. Mind if I come in?"

"Sure," Jack said, stepping aside.

The kid entered and looked around. "Nice place," he said. "A far cry from the officer's barracks."

Jack gestured to the couch. "Thanks. I decided to live off base a few years ago. I recommend it. Have a seat. Care for a cup of coffee?"

"No, thanks. Actually I can't stay long. Anyone here with you, sir?"

"No."

"Good. Well, listen, I just dropped by to see if you were still up for a trip to the moon?"

As these words were being spoken, Muriel Olsen took a seat in Cynthia Weil's office. For this Saturday session, Cynthia was dressed casually, in shorts, tennis shoes and a T-shirt. She had just shared a naughty joke with Muriel – something she did often to break the ice – and noted that it had gotten very little reaction from her patient. Even when not joking, Cynthia had a chatty gift for making therapy sessions into casual conversation. It was through these charismatic personality traits that she had established a warm closeness with Muriel almost at once.

Regardless of her comfort level, however, Muriel was always a little nervous when she first entered Cynthia's office. And this was the case today. She felt the familiar constriction in her throat.

"Well," Cynthia said, "how's it going?"

"Good. I mean everything is falling into place. And he loves me. He really does."

"So that makes you happy, right?"

"Absolutely."

"So why don't I hear that happiness in your voice?"

"I *am* happy.… I just.…"

Cynthia waited, but Muriel didn't continue. "Go on," she finally coaxed. "You just what?"

"I just…I'm not sure. Things just don't seem, I don't know, settled, I guess."

"What's the problem? Jack?"

"No. I don't think so. I mean, he treats me fine and he's an incredibly wonderful man."

"You, then?"

"I don't know…I guess so."

Cynthia chuckled, signaling she wasn't about to accept this answer. "What do you mean, you *guess* so?" she said. "Let's get focused here, kiddo."

"...I just worry."

This was nothing new. Cynthia had heard the same words many times from Muriel. The therapist thought for a moment, then had an idea. "Muriel," she began, "we've been talking a lot over the past few weeks about positive imagery and self confidence techniques."

"And they've helped. They really have. I mean, my outlook now is much more positive."

"Good. But today, just for a few minutes, let's try something different. Instead of all the positive stuff, let's think of the *worst*. Let's say Jack just turned around and walked out of your life forever."

"Wha— But why?"

"Because I want to make a point. If Jack walked out of your life today, Muriel, do you think all the worrying you've done, and all the anxiety you're feeling now, could have changed that?"

"No.... I suppose not."

"Do you think that all the nausea you've talked about and the nightmares could have made him stay if he really wanted to go?"

Muriel looked down, embarrassed. "Of course not," she said.

"So you get it. The pain you've put yourself through hasn't served any *positive* purpose at all. If he were going away, he'd go no matter what you were feeling. We both know that."

Muriel nodded.

"In fact, we've talked about how your negative outlook could even give him a *reason* to leave, remember?"

"Yes."

"I think from what you've told me about Jack he's a very positive guy who wants a positive life. And if you're not able to share in that, if you're not able to help him achieve it, who knows. He might just decide to look elsewhere for someone to share his life with."

Muriel said nothing.

"And if that were the case, if he did decide to walk out of your life today, let me ask again, what would all the misery you've endured have accomplished?"

"…Nothing."

Cynthia moved back to her chair. "Oh, but you're wrong, kiddo," she said, "it *would* have accomplished something. At the very least, it would have spoiled the time you did have with him. And it would have said to him in so many words, 'Pal, this isn't for you. You need to get out – now! You don't need an albatross, you need a mate. See? The future is going to come to pass no matter what happens in your mind and your stomach. No amount of self-torture will change it for the *good*, but it might help change it for the *worse*."

"I know that."

"Okay, then one last time. If your life comes to pass without Jack, what will happen? You'll face it just like you've faced so many other obstacles. You'll survive and you'll go on. It might be sad, but you'll get better and the world won't end, kiddo."

Muriel was quiet again.

"And that's the *worst* possible news. But remember, the worst *isn't the case*, hon — not by a long shot! He loves you. You just said so. He wants to be your husband. He has no intention whatsoever of leaving you. You can accept that and celebrate what a lucky woman you are. In fact, like we've just said, that's the only way you can return Jack's love and really make him happy. You can share all those great dreams of his and all the *good* things in his life. He wants to give those things to you. All you have to do is accept! And to do that, you've got to let go of the fear and self-doubt. You can't give him the love he wants until you can love yourself."

Tears welled up in Muriel's eyes.

"What's keeping that from happening, Muriel?" Cynthia continued. "What's in the way?"

"I've told you."

Cynthia leaned forward. "A bitch of a mother who knocked you around? A father who didn't care all that much about raising a child because he was too busy nursing a bottle and a ruined career? A lonely, insecure childhood? Those are legitimate concerns, hon. They're reasons for you to be here exploring your true feelings and trying to improve your self-esteem. But, sweetheart, they're not that unique. And they're definitely not reasons to jeopardize a relationship with a wonderful man like Jack Moore. They're not a reason to turn him away."

Muriel began to sob. "I know that!" she burst out. "But I can't help it!"

———— •— —• ————

Jack laughed out loud. "Go to the *moon?*", he said.

Darrell threw up his hands. "I know, I know," he said, "it sounds kind of weird. I mean, if you're going to be invited to go to the Moon, you expect it to come from the President, for Christ sakes, or at least a general or someone like that."

"Actually—"

"But its true. There's a mission. It's a once in a lifetime deal. It's happening very fast, it'll take about a month, maybe a little more, and other than that I can only tell you it's about as top secret as they come. Personally, I have no idea what it's about. But I *do* know when things are important. And this one, take my word for it, is *very* important."

As he spoke, Jack realized the kid was for real. His time had come. As bizarre as it seemed, his chance to fly in space had just walked in the front door on the lips of a baby-faced surfer!

His first complete thought, after recovering from the initial shock, was of Muriel. He couldn't go. Their marriage. The future. The way she worried. Her stability.

Then his mind began to race.

It shot back through the years of work and study — the training and conditioning. He remembered floating thirty feet under water in a simulated weightless environment and the overwhelming sense of excitement his first time at the controls of a stealth bomber. He recalled the many wild rides in "Topper", the ASNA centrifuge, jump school, decompression chambers, the simulators — and suddenly he thought of his father. An image came to him of a cold winter night. Jack, a young boy, had been tucked into a sleeping bag, lying on the living room carpet in front of the TV. His father sat on the couch behind him. They watched together as one of many manned space launches lifted off. As the booster climbed through the clouds in a long flaming arc, he recalled his father's words. "You'll get there, Jackie. Be patient. Your turn'll come."

He remembered many other frigid nights he'd spent scanning the skies through the reflector telescope he and his father had made. He'd seen the moons of Jupiter, the rings of Saturn, and craters on the Moon. He recalled, very clearly, dreaming of the day he would touch that soil with his own hands.

Then, out of this stream of memories, came Muriel's face. His fiancée. The woman that had changed his entire perception of manhood and self-worth. The woman he loved and to whom he had made a promise to put aside one set of life dreams to start building another. The woman who was so frail and sensitive and needy. Although the two ideas would have seemed to have clashed, somehow they did not. Jack felt he knew Muriel like he knew himself, and he was absolutely positive that were she standing in front of him at this moment, fearful and insecure as she might be, she would want him to accept. She would insist without question that he go to the moon, get the dream out of his system, then hurry home to marry her and start their new life.

And that's exactly what he decided to do. There was no question of the decision and no more time needed to think it over. He would accept.

The only two problems he foresaw were boarding Cal and letting Muriel know. "I'll go," he said to the kid.

"Great! You know, I kind of figured you'd accept right away."

"When?"

"Now."

"You mean *right* now?"

"Immediately."

Jack looked at Cal. The pup was standing beside the couch, looking quizzically at both men.

"No problem," the kid said, reading Jack's mind. "I'll get him a room at the best pet hotel on the west coast. Red carpet treatment. Promise. Nice looking little guy, by the way. Airedale, isn't he?" As he said this, Darrell dropped to one knee and coaxed Cal toward him. The puppy wagged his stubbed tail and came forward.

"Yes," Jack said. "Four months old."

"What's his name?"

"Cal."

"Cal?"

"Short for Callisto."

Darrell laughed. "A dog named after one of the moons of Jupiter?"

"It seemed right at the time."

Darrell finished petting the dog and got back to his feet. "Well, you can be sure Cal, here, will be given the VIP treatment. That I guarantee."

Cal seemed to like Darrell. He sat between the two men, wagging his tail and looking up.

"There's one other thing," Jack said. "I'd like to call someone."

"Family?"

"No, a friend."

"Sorry, sir."

"She's not even home now. I can leave a message on her machine. It's just that she'll worry if she doesn't at least hear from me."

"Sir, I have very specific orders. On this one, approval by the guys upstairs *before* any contacts are made. And then it's a scripted message, only for immediate family. Sorry. Normally it'd be no problem."

Jack could see that Darrell wasn't about to budge. He also sensed that pushing the issue at this moment was not the right thing to do. "Forget it," he said. "It's not that big a deal. I'll call her when I get the scripted message. Do we take Cal now?"

"Sure. If he doesn't mind the backseat of a Jeep."

Jack picked up and attached Cal's leash. Darrell started out the door. When he was on the porch, Jack stopped. "Hang on," he said. "Quick pit stop — unless that's a no-no, too."

"Sure thing," Darrell said, pausing slightly. Jack passed the young man Cal's leash and walked into his bedroom. Darrell quickly inched forward so he could see into the room. Jack stepped into the bathroom and closed the door. As he urinated he took a pen from his pocket. He scratched a quick note to Muriel on a torn off piece of a deodorant box cover. He flushed the toilet, quickly folded the note and tucked it up under his belt. He then stepped out of the bathroom, noticing that Darrell gave him a quick once-over and seemed satisfied.

The two headed for the front door. Jack took Cal's leash again. As he was pulling the door closed he quickly reached under his belt and popped the note out onto the carpet.

He closed the door and they left.

FIFTEEN

Muriel became concerned when Jack was ten minutes late at the mall. He was never late. She immediately began to pace in front of the Acapulco Terrace, the Mexican restaurant where they'd planned to meet. She looked up and down both sides of the mall several times, hoping to see him approaching among the shopping crowds. When fifteen minutes had passed, she became frightened. She took out her cell phone, called his apartment and got his machine. She tried his cell. It went straight to Voicemail. She waited another fifteen minutes, reasoning that maybe he'd gotten a flat or had been called into some special meeting. Finally, after ten more minutes, she rushed out of the mall and sped off to his apartment.

She knocked and got no answer.

Using her key she opened the door and stepped in. She called out, but got no response. She went quickly from room to room, checking every detail of everything she observed. His computer on. iPAD on the coffee table. Paperwork on his desk. Dirty socks sticking out of the clothes hamper. A computer manual lying open. A half done Sudoku puzzle. Warm coffee still in the pot. No Cal.… *No Cal?*

She felt the first sickening waves of panic begin to tighten in her stomach. After another walk through the apartment, she was making the final decision to call the air base when she returned to the living room. It was then that she noticed the torn, folded piece of box cover on the carpet beside the leg of an end table.

She picked it up, unfolded it, and read:

Sweetheart,
Have to leave. Maybe a month. Finally!
The Dream! Be back soon. <u>Love you!</u>
J

She was relieved at first. At least he hadn't left her. Thank God! At least he still loved her. He hadn't just walked out of her life. Or had he? What would call him away for a month with no notice? Was it the first step in a plan to leave her for good? No, she decided. He *did* love her. He had said so. He had proposed. She had his ring to prove it. She grasped and held the diamond tightly between her fingers. And those words, "Finally! The Dream!" Finally what? What dream? A space flight? Unsure of exactly what to think, Muriel sat on the couch and went through every possibility she could imagine. A call to work, a secret mission, a joke, abandonment.… The more she thought, the more the possibilities became negative and threatening. She called his office and got an assistant.

"Lieutenant Colonel Moore, please."

"Sorry, ma'am he's not in today."

"You're sure he hasn't been called in?"

"Let me check.… No, Ma'am, he's not in."

Fifteen minutes later she began to cry and she was still crying when she found herself back in Cynthia's office.

"Did you two have a fight or something?" were the first words out of Cynthia's mouth.

"No," Muriel sobbed, "I didn't even see him. There was just this note!" She produced the now crumpled piece of box and gave it to Cynthia.

The moment Cynthia looked at it she sighed. "Well, it's obvious, Muriel! He's on a mission! Some secret military thing. And he says he loves you! It's okay, kid! Out of, what, about ten words here, he's said he loves you and he even underlined it, for God's sake. You should be happy for him!"

"I am, but—"

"Hon, this is probably the best thing that could have happened."

"Why?" Muriel sobbed.

"Because now, hopefully, he's getting this thing out of his system. I'll bet his mission really did come through, and he'll be able to fulfill that dream before you and he settle down. Don't you see? It just might be exactly what the doctor ordered."

Muriel began to feel better.

"But you've got to be tough, kid and resolute. You've got to stick it out for a few weeks and do just what he's asked — trust in him."

"You're right."

"Of course I'm right."

Muriel was regaining her composure. "I'll do fine," she said. "I can do it. I love him and he loves me and I know it'll be okay."

"Can you handle being alone?"

"Yes."

"Are you sure?"

"Positive."

"Listen," Cynthia said, "things aren't that busy for me right now, so you call me. Understand? We can always powwow over the phone."

"Yes," Muriel said, thankfully. "I will — maybe more than you'll care for."

"Anytime. I'm not kidding. Day or night. Even for lunch or something. I'm always available — especially if you start again with the nightmares."

"Okay."

Cynthia held Muriel's shoulders and leveled her gaze directly into the frightened woman's eyes. "Listen to me. You're making exceptional progress. You're on the threshold of a wonderful new time in your life. Think about that. You're finally at the door!"

Muriel nodded, sobbing lightly.

"I've helped you get this far, and I feel damn good about that. And I don't want this to set back all the work we've done."

"Okay."

"Then you'll call if you need help?"

"Yes."

"Okay. And if I don't hear from you, I'll see you next week, bright and early."

The weariness that was part of her darkness seemed to be growing very slowly. And this had some relationship to the pounding and shaking and the pulling downward on the most dense parts of her.

There was no thought of stopping.

The question of whether or not to continue, like the very language and intellect she lacked, simply did not exist. She would go on, weary or not, because that, too — that long, tiring, continuous motion — was as much a part of her as the darkness itself.

The panic inside her was growing more intense, but oddly, so, too, was the sense of hope. And somewhere deep in her being she had some form of mathematical memory that said this had all happened before. She had approached some source and it had intensified all parts of the darkness — but most of all the panic and the hope.

She was sure it had happened, not once or twice, but many times. But somehow she had never managed to quite reach those sources. In every case a kind of change had come and the question of hope had remained unanswered.

Something would always move inside of her. Though she had no control over it, some priority would shift — some polarity suddenly reverse. And when it happened, all focus would move to another place inside her and she would have to slow the pounding and the shaking and regain a sense of exactly where inside her things were happening. During these times she recalled the weariness and pulling downward would decrease.

But then, having gained some new perspective, some new purpose or direction, it would all begin again.

Over and over.

Time after time.

The panic, the fear, the pounding and pulling and the elusive thread of hope.

And beneath all this, the one unchanging part of the darkness was her need. Regardless of her position or movement, regardless of all other factors, the constant desire for some connection to another being, the intense belief that it would be fulfilled, kept its place inside her.

SIXTEEN

The morning after his visit by Darrell Coenan, Jack Moore sat together with two other officers in a small, plush classroom on the fourth floor of Section 13-A at Saltridge.

The man beside Jack was Colonel Allan Tiller, a thin, square-jawed, flat-topped commander with a deep, gravelly, Texas drawl. Across from Jack and Tiller sat Captain Janice Polling, a young, bright-eyed, blond woman who reminded Jack somewhat of a female Darrell Coenan. The group had just made introductions at breakfast and it was obvious that all had gotten pretty well the same offer as Jack — a top secret trip to the moon; an on-the-spot decision required; notification to no one.

The room was oval in shape with a mauve carpeted floor and high ceilings. At its center sat a long, rosewood table at which the astronauts sat, accompanied by a video projector and a stack of electronic gear. One of the side walls was dominated by a five by seven foot rectangular white board. A large plasma screen had been built into the front center wall and several smaller screens were mounted around the room. An easel had been provided at the front left. Coffee and pitchers of juice and water had been placed at the far end of the table along with a tray of fruit, yogurt and Danish. At the rear of the room were two large globes — one of the earth, the other of the moon. Each was roughly three feet in diameter and both stood on identical, carved wooden pedestals on either side of an arrangement of antique shelves. On the shelves were volumes of astronomical and aeronautical books. A variety of lush, leafy plants had been placed generously around the room, providing a pleasant visual accent to the already attractive environment.

At the head of the room stood John Pike, an Air Force major and genetic scientist. He had just introduced himself and told the three astronauts he would supervise the training they would receive during the initial days of their stay at Saltridge.

Pike was a plump, balding man with bright, white hair and a shiny, round face. He wore large, thin framed, designer glasses with lenses much too thick to look chic. Though the combination of his plump frame, stark white hair and "hip" glasses made him appear almost comical, the astronauts had read on his bio sheet that he was considered a foremost authority in the field of genetic mapping and exploration.

Jack studied Pike carefully as the portly major approached the conclusion of his opening remarks. "...and I'm told you've been given a firm launch date of the

27th. Due to the secrecy of the mission, you will remain here in isolation for the entire training and orientation period - the majority of which, as I just mentioned, you will spend under my supervision. So, I believe that introduces us, and explains our charter for the next several days. Any questions?"

"When do we get the full scoop?" Tiller said.

"Starting right now. Anything else before we dig in?"

The group remained quiet.

"Fine, then I'd like to wrap up this little introduction of mine by saying that I am extremely proud to be a part of this mission. You officers have been handpicked to participate in what may be the most critical moon landing in the history of space travel. Paradoxically, however, it's a mission that will get the least amount of fanfare. In fact, it will get none. Only a small group of individuals even know of the existence of "Operation Round-Up" and you'll be working directly with fewer still."

He keyed several strokes into his laptop and picked up a remote control. The large plasma screen at the head of the room lit up. On it, the title *Operation Round-Up* appeared. "Now then, put all this together on a short fuse and you can imagine how little time we have to waste." The lights dimmed. "So," he continued, "I'll get right down to business."

As Pike now began clicking through a PowerPoint slide presentation, an image appeared on the screen. It was a simple illustration that looked something like a coiled yellow spiral staircase with rows of multi-colored balls and bars forming each of the "steps". He turned to the men. "Let's start with the letters, D.N.A.," he said. "What do they mean?"

Jack spoke up. "I can't give you the full scientific name but we all know DNA is the basic building material of life. It's made up of protein molecules arranged in a kind of coiled ladder — the double helix, shown up there."

Pike smiled. "Exactly," he said. "The letters D.N.A. stand for Deoxyribonucleic Acid, by the way. And you're right, Jack, it's a pretty familiar term these days, especially with all the press on cloning and the mapping of the human genome. But how about some specifics? Just what are the rungs and joints in the DNA ladder, and what do they determine?"

After a moment of hesitation, Tiller spoke. "Our physical make-up — color of hair and eyes, physical features –- that kind of stuff."

"Right again," Pike said.

He moved forward to the edge of the table in front of the men. "DNA determines virtually *everything* physical, and much mental, about us - from the charge capacity of the neurons in our brains to the pigment of our skin, and curl and length of our eyelashes."

He stepped back to the laptop. "And it makes these determinations not just for us humans, or even just for everything in the animal kingdom. DNA is the most basic building block of every living thing, from the cells in blades of grass to the texture of an elephant's skin. It is quite simply the descriptive material of all existence."

He looked at Jack. "And your choice of the word 'ladder' was, as we are able to see here, Jack, a good one — a multi-faceted, spiral ladder made up of numerous, precise combinations of molecular amino acids."

He pulled a laser pointer from his pocket, clicked, and placed the red dot on the connection at a rung. "A ladder in which the placement of molecular rungs determine some characteristic of the organism. Here, for instance, one tiny piece of the organic puzzle that determines perhaps blue rather than hazel color to the iris of the eye."

He pointed to another rung. "And here, perhaps one aspect of the determination of fingers instead of claws. And here, possibly an arm the size and shape of a man's rather than the dorsal fin of, say, a killer whale."

As if to let the importance of what he was saying sink in, he paused and stared at the group for a long moment. "And specifically how," he finally asked, "do all these rungs and joints and protein molecules end up in the right order?"

"Duplication through normal cell reproduction," Polling said.

Again the scientist seemed pleased. "Right, Janice. We know that as the cells of a living organism reproduce, the chromosomes in those cells, which are essentially bundles of DNA, are able to make identical, perfectly arranged genetic copies of themselves. Or, in the case of cells from two organisms combining during the reproduction process, such as the male sperm and female egg, the combination of chromosomes, and thus DNA, from both organisms. But they're still arranged to assure that an eye remains an eye, even if the shape and color of that eye is determined by the dominant of the two genes."

Again Pike paused. Jack thought he seemed to be searching for a choice of words. "But the question of how all these building blocks end up in just the right order," he said, "raises an interesting consideration — our ability to *rearrange* or replace certain rungs or joints."

The room was still. Jack sensed something new in Pike's demeanor. Out of the corner of his eye he glanced at the others. Polling fidgeted in her seat. Tiller was chewing a toothpick.

"Today," Pike continued, "we are able to alter the physical and to some degree the mental make up of many living organisms. You've all heard of Dolly the sheep and other more recent cloning successes like stem cell regeneration. And there are many much less talked about accomplishments taking place as we speak, in the science of genetic manipulation."

He referred again to the plasma screen with his laser. "Perhaps a blue cat's eye here, where once the ladder had determined a brown human eye should go... Here the replacement of, say, a coccyx stub with a full prehensile tail... Four human arms here, where there were supposed to have been two..."

Jack noticed that the new change in Pike was intensifying as he spoke. He almost seemed to be getting excited, as if he were coming to the punch line of a great joke. "In fact," he continued, "take that thought a step farther. Imagine we are not only able to arrange or substitute rungs at will, but also that we are able to...*create* ncw rungs."

All three astronauts sat quietly.

"Suppose we could manufacture this stuff of life and arrange the rungs in a form that would meet the needs of, say, a 200 year space exploration. And suppose this exploration was to be carried out in a craft with a control panel that required an individual with half a dozen arms and no legs."

"Let me get this straight," Jack said, "Are you telling us that organic life *has* actually been created in the laboratory? And if so, and I'm reading all this right, it has something to do with this mission?"

Another of Pike's long silences followed. Finally he picked up his remote control. He turned up all the room lights and moved back to the front center of the table.

"Are any of you men familiar with the name Andrew Weincamp?" he asked.

Polling answered. "Who isn't. He's the scientist that just committed murder and suicide."

Tiller picked up on the thought. "Yeah. Didn't the news reports say he was working on some space project?"

"Right," Pike said, "the effects of deep space radiation on chromosome and cell reproduction — or so the world thought."

Pike placed his pointer down and checked his watch. "It occurs to me," he said, "this conversation would be best continued in a lab environment. But first I have a few arrangements to make. You'll find coffee and juice in room 1-B. Let's meet again in twenty minutes in room 14-C, two levels down."

Then he turned and left the room.

SEVENTEEN

Room 1-B was much like the classroom.

The moment Jack entered it he thought to himself it resembled an elegant hotel dining room. Three tables and four booths sat on the green carpeting and the walls were covered with framed copies of historic military documents. A small tile fountain stood at the center of the room with a decorative fern centerpiece.

Trellised and potted plants hung from rustic beams along with decorative chandeliers. An elaborate spread of rolls, breads and fruit lay terraced on a long table with a red and yellow tablecloth. On an adjacent table, the group found a display of juices, coffees and several varieties of teas and sodas packed in ice.

Jack poured himself a cup of decaf. As he finished, a news segment on a large TV mounted in the corner of the room caught his eye. He turned to hear Martin Balk formally announce his candidacy for the presidency.

In his smooth, impeccable manner the Vice President was saying, "...and I agree that what America needs now is a sense of unity and increased innovation. But we also have to show great care in how we infuse those elements into the fabric of our society. We must also remember we have a budget — a price to pay — and I'm afraid many of my Democratic friends remain oblivious to this fact of life. What I continue to see are their usual attempts to pour money over every problem America has in the hope we can simply drown out solutions. The truth is, solutions cannot be bought, they must be earned. Earned with plain old hard work and patriotism. That's what has always worked for this great country, and that's exactly what will work during my term in office as your President."

As the applause went up, Jack chuckled and thought to himself, *the perfect politician — smooth, convincing, political B.S.*

Tiller must have been moved by Balk's words. He filled his cup beside Jack, saying, "'At's the guy I'm votin' for, Jack. No bullshit. No pussyfootin' around with these damned Democrats. He knows what this country needs. You ain't a Democrat are you, Jack?"

Jack smiled. Not wanting to start a political or ideological discussion just as the two were getting acquainted, he simply said, "It's going to be an interesting election year. I'm looking forward to it."

"Me too, Jack," Tiller said. "Looking forward to doin' in these damn Democrats."

"Speaking of being done in," Jack said, "how about this scientist, Andrew Weincamp?"

Just then Polling stepped up munching an apple.

"Bizarre," she said. "I mean, what makes a guy with those kinds of credentials walk into a confessional, blow away a priest, then chuck his own brains all over the walls?"

"That's what I'd like to know," Jack said. "Sounds screwy."

"Went off the deep end," Tiller spouted, as if there were no doubt whatsoever.

"I did hear he was a drinker," Polling added.

The three moved to a nearby table. "Not too un-usual with guys like him," Tiller continued. "They're so fuckin' smart they're damn near whacko. Has a little setback in his work or somethin', starts to come a little unraveled, that leads to more trouble in the lab, he gets into a bad cycle, and, 'fore you know it, only one way out… Boom!"

EIGHTEEN

Twenty minutes later the group stepped into room 14-C, a large, immaculate lab.

Pike began at once providing answers.

He started with the question Jack had asked earlier. "Yes, Jack," he said, "thanks to Andrew Weincamp's research we have actually created life, or something very much like it. A version of life, I should say, and yes, it has everything to do with this mission."

He led the men around a corner and down a long, white tiled corridor. At the end of the corridor the group turned another corner and found themselves beside a large caged off area topped by a huge skylight.

The massive bars of the cage looked like two inch brushed steel. They created a metal face some twenty feet high and forty feet long. Inside were half-buried stumps of telephone poles connected by thick ropes, leafy vegetation, granite blocks and even several tractor tires lying in the dirt. Adjacent to the caged area were several chairs and tables and an array of electronic control equipment, most of which was built into the opposite wall.

A huge animal cage in the middle of a place like Saltridge seemed odd to Jack by itself, but when he looked carefully inside he was even more shocked. Lying in an immaculately groomed grassy area, amongst a cluster of surrounding bushes and ledges was a full grown silverback gorilla. Even more peculiar was the totally unnatural way it was lying — on its stomach with both arms and legs spread eagle.

Jack had never seen any animal lay like this, and the sight of it at first made him think the gorilla was dead.

Tiller made the same assumption, "Dead?" he asked Pike.

"No," Pike responded. "As a matter of fact he's just resting. His name is Howie, by the way, and he's a six hundred and twenty pound African Silverback gorilla."

Pike paused and glanced at each of the officers to get their reactions. All three appeared mesmerized. "I'd say," he continued, "he's just about had enough of his morning nap. I'm about to wake him. But before I do, I want you to look closely at his back — the area between his right shoulder and the base of his neck."

All eyes looked immediately. Jack saw a lump — a muscle, he thought at first. But he quickly realized it was too large and seemed to be positioned in the wrong way for a muscle. Pike continued, "Do you all see the lump there?"

Everyone acknowledged.

"Good. Keep an eye on it." As he said this he moved to the electronic panel area and began to enter a series of commands into a computer keyboard.

At first the lump seemed to contract. Then it quivered slightly and finally it appeared to swell. At the same time Howie stirred. Seconds later he rolled over on his side, moved to a seated position, and sat motionless, staring out at the group.

"I'll be darned!" Polling whispered.

"As you may all suspect," Pike said, "the lump on Howie's shoulder is very special. Actually it's a man-made organ."

"How does it work?" Tiller asked.

"It's function is to translate multi-frequency, digital sound transmissions into chemical and hormonal secretions."

"And you're providing the transmissions with the computer?" Jack asked.

"Exactly."

For some reason, perhaps because of her inability to fully comprehend Howie, Polling chuckled nervously. In a half joking tone she blurted out, "Hah! Does he do tricks?"

Pike seemed a bit irritated by the young captain's lack of seriousness, but he answered the question. "Actually, Janice, we can make Howie do almost anything. You see, different frequencies, pulse rates and amplitudes cause him to experience different emotional reactions."

For several seconds the group said nothing. All simply stared. Finally Pike continued, "The tissue in that lump is man-made. It's just one example of Andrew Weincamp's life work."

"How can flesh — man-made or not — react to sound waves?" Jack asked.

"Think of the sound in terms of stimulation," Pike said. As he said this he keyed more information into the computer and continued, "For instance..."

Suddenly Howie leaped onto all fours and let out a tremendous roar. Moore, Tiller and Polling immediately jumped backward.

Pike continued his sentence. "...you all reacted to that sound, didn't you? Besides jumping nearly out of your pants, your pulses quickened and no doubt the hair on the backs of your necks stood up, as well."

"Emotional responses," Jack said, half to himself.

"Right, Jack, caused by chemical secretions as a result of very high frequency audio stimulation. That's a gross over-simplification, of course, but you get the point."

Polling chuckled again nervously, shook her head and this time whispered to Tiller, "And now ladies and gentlemen..."

Tiller chuckled. Pike heard the comment and once again eyed Polling.

He then went on to key information into the computer which made Howie pick up a clump of bamboo and begin to munch. Several minutes later he made the gorilla lose his computer generated appetite and drop the shoots. When not involved in an activity Pike was generating for him, Howie sat quietly staring at the group.

Jack was both fascinated and repulsed by what he was seeing. He knew full well that animal cloning and experimentation went on continually and some of what was done was downright barbaric. But to make an animal almost 'robotic', that seemed even more inhumane somehow. It was bad enough to torture an animal in the name of science, but to also enslave its mind?

As he was considering this thought, Polling put her foot in her mouth a final time. She shook her head again and with an awkward, half smile on her face turned to Jack and said, "Hey, Robo-rilla!"

"You know, Janice," Pike said, "I don't think movie names are in order, but Howie hasn't…" he began keying information into the computer, "…blown off any steam in quite a while."

Suddenly Howie tensed and snapped his head around toward the group – Polling, it seemed, in particular. "I think we'll make him mad… mad at…" he keyed more information in, "…you, Janice."

Howie lowered his head and seemed to look directly at Polling. The hair on the back of his neck stood up. He began to slink forward slowly, methodically, like a stalking lion.

Pike continued to key in data. "That should be pretty…entertaining…huh, Janice?" he said jovially.

Suddenly, Howie's huge fangs barred like a dog's. He growled, moved forward, and lowered his head even more. Tiller and Jack both began to inch backward. Polling looked quickly at the others as if seeking help. She, too, began to back away.

Pike keyed in the final bit of information, and with a smile said, "Should be a real crowd pleaser!"

Suddenly Howie exploded forward in a thunderous rage, directly toward Polling. His roar was deafening.

He slammed against the bars with an impact that could have demolished the wall of a house. As his squat, six hundred pound body crashed into the steel, the entire room quaked. His huge black hands and hairy arms reached through the bars, straining to grasp and tear at Polling's face, to clutch her hair, rip her face open... reaching...straining...

NINETEEN

…to get free. But it did her no good. As always in the dream, it surrounded her like a straight jacket, enclosing her and holding her arms close to her body.

In the beginning Muriel never knew quite what it was. There was just some presence, some evil weight that was part of the darkness, and the air, and everything in existence.

This time she was running down a corridor with a shiny, sunlit floor. She turned around and felt ashes spewing from her mouth. A thin, homely nurse stood by a drinking fountain and laughed at her. As Muriel tried to edge past the woman an invisible presence flashed in her eyes. Liquid dripped from the old woman's mouth down onto her wrinkled chin.

Muriel fell on the shiny floor and rolled over onto a wide, grass expanse. She tried to gain her feet but couldn't. Her legs were heavy and slow and sinking into the mulchy ground. She tried to use her arms to get to her feet but something held them at her sides. The grass was turning to mud — warm, slippery, deep, dangerous mud. She struggled to free herself, but couldn't budge. She turned and beside her was a marble grave marker with no name on it. Something held her. Something alive. Something dead...

And then came the hands, and a blinding sun above her.

Droplets of warm, smelly water fell on her face, and a buzzing of whispers and music and grunting sounds blared in the distance.

The hands touched her. There was an evil coldness and hardness about them. They kneaded her face and breasts. They moved over her body slowly and found her throat, and then they began to tighten. She struggled to breathe. Suddenly they loosened and moved downward to her stomach.

The sun came down closer to her eyes — or was it the moon? Its intense brilliance burned fiercely.

Muriel could feel hysteria rising up in her mind.

The hands moved over her slowly. She tried to reach them, to hold them off, but she seemed to have no hands herself.

The sun (the moon?) burned into her face and the hands took hold of her stomach. She tried to get up off the bed, but she couldn't, and the hands were pushing through her skin.

The sensation was painless, but horrifying — like having her soul bathed in diseased water. Waves of repulsion swept through her like a strong, sour wind. A hot current of panic dumped out of the blinding light.

And the hands were inside her, sloshing through organs, grasping at her spine.

Then, as always in this dream, the hands were suddenly gone and the light began to dim.

But they had succeeded and she knew that.

She was no longer Muriel Olsen. She had become another person — a stranger that had knowledge of, or connection to, Muriel. It was this horrible realization that made her scream and suddenly come to a sitting position — fully awake, on her bed.

In the other room, her refrigerator was humming. The clock read 2:45 A.M. Her throat had almost entirely closed. She wheezed and felt the panic coming, rising up, taking her mind out of her body. She struggled to hold it, to keep her sanity.

She got up from her bed, turned on the light, and ran to the kitchen. She opened the refrigerator, knelt in front of it and began talking up into the cold white light. "Muriel," she said, "you are just fine. You just need to stop thinking about this and have a snack. You need some...some milk, young lady... Milk...It does a body good. ..and you are going to be good — just fine. The thing is, kiddo, you need some cookies. And...God, you've just got to hold on!"

TWENTY

At seven A.M. Jack, Tiller, and Polling were back in the conference room.

Pike was at the head of the oval table discussing Andrew Weincamp's research. "The world thought he was working on the effects of deep space on chromosome reproduction," he said. "But the fact is, Weincamp was creating life — life that could help man explore the farthest reaches of space — life that could survive in the most hostile environments and extreme temperatures. Life that didn't depend on the essential elements which are nowhere to be found within light years of us — oxygen, water and organic food materials. A kind of life that was totally new to our thinking as human beings."

Jack felt he already knew the answer to the question he was about to ask. "And was he successful?"

Pike opened the laptop and dimmed the lights. As he did this he said, "Yes, Jack, he was. The environment he chose was the closest, most accessible one that provided many of the characteristics he was after — the moon. And the life form he chose," Pike continued, "was Moonmare."

As he said this he brought a graphic animator's rendition of Moonmare onto the screen. She was rendered as an animal that appeared to be a cross between a horse and an elephant. She was shown standing on what appeared to be a lunar landscape. Beside her, to give relationship to her size, was an image of an astronaut in a life support suit. The top of the astronaut's helmet came to about the animal's chest

"What the hell is she?" Tiller asked, flipping a toothpick over his tongue to the side of his mouth.

Again Jack noticed that Pike seemed to become excited. "She's like nothing you've ever imagined," he said.

"Looks like an oversized horse to me," Polling said.

"A little overweight, too," Tiller added with a chuckle. "Actually," Pike continued, "she looks like those things on the outside. But that's where the similarity ends – with physical shape."

"She's not part horse?" Jack asked.

"Some of the Actol-YL DNA she's made of was replicated, not from a horse, actually, but from a zebra."

"Actol-YL DNA?" Jack probed.

"Right. Weincamp's version of the molecular DNA ladder structure we talked about yesterday. A version made, not from the organic material we know as common to our existence — proteins, fats, sugars and amino acids — but from a totally new substance created in the lab. A kind of super space DNA."

"So she's not even really an animal?" Polling asked.

"No, she's not. She simply *appears* in animal form because that happens to be the shape that best suits the needs of her existence."

"And she's up on the moon right now?" Tiller asked, looking amazed.

"Exactly."

Jack thought about Howie, the gorilla. A twinge of that same basic repulsion, born out of the thought of animal torture and control, rose up in his stomach. This led to thoughts of Cal. How was he doing? Was he really getting the so called V.I.P treatment? Was he lonely, lying in some strange kennel? Did he think Jack had abandoned him?

Pike turned and dropped the artist's rendition. A segment of actual video footage of Moonmare appeared on the screen. "These were taken roughly a month ago from an orbiting EOS module," Pike said. "They're not great, but they'll at least give you some idea of what she looks like in the... "flesh", so to speak. We've been having some troubles with the LMOS, so these were the last we've seen of her. And I'm afraid they're the last we'll get — at least for the moment, that is."

The images were dark and grainy. Because they were shot from directly overhead, at extremely high magnification, and the mare's color closely resembled the surrounding lunar terrain, it was difficult to make out her features. In addition, the images were tiny, and some were even blotched. Her overall shape, however, and some minor details were visible. Jack noted what seemed to be a round wide body and a pale rump. On one of the clearest segments she appeared to have been in full gallop. Small nubs, which Jack assumed were her hooves, appeared to poke out from the area of her head and rump.

Next Pike put up an artist's cross-section of Moon-mare. It showed nothing like one normally sees inside an animal - stomach, intestines, lungs and so on. There was a skeleton, which Jack assumed wasn't made of real bone, a muscular structure, and several organs. Two were large and prominent.

The largest was in the area that would normally be the brain. It didn't look like a brain, however. It was cubed in shape and fissured with hundreds of tiny arced slits that formed patterns on it like a covering of gills. It was connected to the spine, however, as was the second one. This one was at the opposite end of the body, just under the spine, where a normal horse's colon would be. It, too, was cubed and covered in patterns, but these were more honeycombed, like a beehive.

"As you can see," Pike continued, "she has two brains. The emotional one at the head of her spine helps us motivate her. The logical brain at the opposite end serves one of the real reasons for her existence."

"Which is?" Jack asked.

"To return geographical data about the surface of the moon — something she's been doing successfully for the last six months."

Jack was having trouble with the entire concept. "But how does she exist, John. I mean, you're talking about temperatures up there of 130 degrees centigrade during the day and -170 at night! No oxygen, no food. What keeps her moving?"

Pike pointed out several clusters of small organs connected like grapes along the length of Moonmare's spine. "These," he said. "They're very similar to the organ you saw yesterday on Howie's shoulder. We send a beam of combined, high speed, multi-frequency sound transmissions from here at Saltridge to the moon. Since it forms a kind of lifeline for her, we call it the Umbilical. It's multitude of tone and frequency patterns stimulates these organs and provides Moonmare everything she needs to exist and function — instructions, the equivalent of nutrition, oxygen, balance, coordination, temperature control — basically everything she needs to move around and communicate with us."

Pike pointed to another organ near the end of the spine. It was larger than the "grape" clusters, but smaller than the two brains. It was butterfly shaped. "And over here," he said, "is her means of sending back data along that same beam. This organ receives information collected by her logical brain — information about her surrounding terrain, temperature fluctuations, ground compaction and so on. It changes that information into digital radio transmissions and utilizes a frequency range on the beam to send the data back to earth. It's a kind of special Moonmare language, you might say."

"She talks?" Polling asked.

"Well, yes, but not in what you and I would consider normal words, or even animal sounds. She simply sends back a stream of digital information. It's fed through a decoder program designed to convert the information into data we can translate — a kind of human computer language created from numbers."

"Where exactly is she on the moon?" Jack asked.

"In a very large, generally circular area on the backside."

"Why the backside?"

"We'll get into that in-depth tomorrow, Jack. For the moment, let's just say for privacy sake. Remember, she's top secret."

Tiller pulled his toothpick from his mouth and leaned forward. Jack could see he was about to pose one of those questions meant to 'stump' the professor. "And just how in hell do you keep her there? That's what I want to know. And don't tell me you got some two thousand square mile barbed wire fence up there."

"No Al, no fence," Pike said with a chuckle. "At least not in a physical sense."

He brought up another image. It was a map of the area where Moonmare was kept. Surrounding the area was an oval ring of blue dots with sequential letter/number combinations next to each dot.

The sequence began with the upper most dot. It was labeled "C-1". To its right was "C-2", then came "C-3" and so on creating an oval. The final blue dot, which was to the left of the first, was labeled "C-14".

"C," Pike said, "stands for Caller."

At the sound of the word, the repulsion surfaced again in Jack.

"You see," Pike said to Tiller, "the question you raised, Al, was a very legitimate concern during Moonmare's development. How to keep her in a certain area or motivate her to, say, change direction. How do you get her to go where you want? This network of fourteen Callers provide the solution to that problem. They were put in place with a fleet of top secret, unmanned craft – specifically equipped landers, that positioned the Callers on the surface and actually self-drilled parts of their structures into the lunar terrain. The Callers, too, are controlled from this installation. When activated they emit a series of vibrations that travel through the lunar soil to Moonmare's location. She senses the vibrations and is...motivated, to move in that direction."

"So, by turning these things on and off," Tiller assumed out loud, "you can make her go in any direction you want."

"Right, Al."

"Kind of like a dog called to a whistle," Polling said.

Pike hesitated. Jack noted that he seemed just a bit uncomfortable with this analogy. "Well, not exactly, Janice," he said, "but generally speaking, yes."

Jack sensed something about the question was troubling Pike. He decided to pursue it. "Just how do these, Callers differ from a dog's attraction to a whistle?"

Again, Pike hesitated. "That's another subject we'll cover in more detail later, but for now let me say that a dog's attraction to a whistle is basically a learned response — something Weincamp didn't have the luxury of in Moonmare's case. Second, it's not a guaranteed response. For instance, suppose something else gets the dog's attention as he's coming in toward the whistle? He could break from his direction completely."

"Not a whole lot of things to break attention on the backside of the moon," Polling said with a smile.

"You're right, Janice, but none the less a *guaranteed* response was required before Moonmare could actually become a reality."

"And just how did Weincamp get that guarantee?" Jack asked.

After a moment to ponder the question and, Jack felt, choose his words carefully, Pike answered. "He found he had to incorporate the equivalent of very basic instincts. There were two choices — survival and reproduction. Had Weincamp chosen reproduction, Moonmare would now be interpreting the Caller's vibrations as, say, the mating call of a male creature like herself."

"So she'd be horny as hell and running around up there tryin' to find this stud pony," Tiller said, spitting out the toothpick.

"Right. But when you get right down to it, although the desire to reproduce is a basic and very powerful instinctive force, it, too, cannot provide a complete guarantee. Survival, on the other hand, does just that. So, in the end, that's what Weincamp chose. Exactly how that works you'll see soon enough."

TWENTY-ONE

Muriel stood at the window in Cynthia's office staring out at traffic passing on a nearby freeway overpass. She had just made a tearful confession to the psychologist.

Cynthia's voice came from behind her. "You've got to talk to him," she said. "You've got to come up front and get all this off your chest, just like you finally did with me. And you also have to make that trip. You need release, kid, and you need it right now."

"I may never see him again!" Muriel sobbed.

"Don't be silly. He wrote to you he'd be home in a few weeks and he *will* be. He loves you."

Muriel turned from the window, crossed the room, and sat across from Cynthia. "How do you tell the man who has become your entire life, the man who has placed you on this throne of perfection, that you're not perfect at all. In fact, you're pretty darned tarnished."

Cynthia leaned in and took Muriel's hands. Muriel had begun to sob. "The question is not how do you tell him, hon. It's how can you possibly go on with your life and this relationship *without* telling him. Let's face it, you're a wreck and you need to get this off your back, period!"

"But will he still want me?"

"Muriel, the man who wrote that note I saw a few days ago has no choice. He loves you, and honey, you've got him right where it counts! Remember, this is a man willing to redirect his entire life for the love of a woman. A man ready to give up his career and aspirations, for God sakes, just for you! Do you really think he could leave you because of things you couldn't control? Because you're not some perfect little 'porcelain doll'? C'mon, Muriel… "

"I guess you're right."

"Of course, I'm right. And I'll tell you what else I'm right about. The minute you resolve this — take that ride, and talk to Jack — or even just *decide* to talk to him — these nightmares are going to stop."

Muriel thought of the dream. The panic welled up in her again. She got to her feet and again moved to the window. As she walked she closed her eyes and whispered to herself, "Hang on, kid."

The sunlight and activity outside were good —distracting. An elderly lady started out across a crosswalk on a small electric cart. A delivery truck pulled up at the curb. Three Girl Scouts skipped along on the sidewalk. She felt herself relax. "God, I hope so," she said.

"Do you want to talk about them today?"

"No...I don't know...I just, I just get overwhelmed by this...this sensation that there's no hope or forgiveness."

Cynthia held Muriel's shoulders. "Go ahead," she said quietly as Muriel began to cry.

TWENTY-TWO

The Bell R-22 Beta II helicopter lifted off from Helipad 2-ABEL beside the Saltridge observatory. Pike took the craft to seven hundred feet, veering northeast, away from Highway 10. It was a hot, sunny day and the chopper passed over acres of parched, desert terrain spotted with rocks, scrubby bush and cacti.

As the bright, hot sand passed below, Jack thought to himself that the desert had a kind of magical, unnoticed simplicity — a wonderful openness and calm that he knew could be found in no other type of landscape. He thought of Muriel, his decision to take the mission, Moonmare…

Minutes later a ridge of mountains appeared on the horizon to the east. Pike banked toward it. "It's just over that small range," he hollered over the rotor's blast.

A few minutes later, as the aircraft passed above a spine of rocky, barren peaks, Jack's jaw dropped. Below them on the desert floor were large herds of animals. Pike gestured toward the herds.

"Welcome, gentlemen," he said, "to Andrew Weincamp's little Africa."

Below them were hundreds of African plains animals — wildebeest, large and small gazelle, gnu and various other grazers. "Holy shit," Tiller said. "Time for the round up!"

"Any ticked-off gorillas down there?" Polling quipped.

Pike and Polling laughed.

Jack saw that Pike was headed for a herd of zebra. "Weincamp had to do extensive research during the development of Moonmare," he said. "After some initial processes of elimination he knew he would need to borrow characteristics from some of the African plains animals."

"Why was that?" Jack hollered.

"Because he knew she would be doing lots of running. She'd have to cover large areas of the moon in order to return the data required. Going to Africa for an extended period just wasn't practical, so, Uncle Sam brought Africa to him."

"How big is it?" Polling asked.

"Six-hundred and twenty-thousand acres. Entirely fenced off and known as a private wildlife preserve under government regulation. Part of the so-called 'Save the Species' program that originated a decade ago."

Jack remembered the program. It had been billed as a way to breed African wildlife in an ecosystem similar to their own in order to study their life cycles and thus help preserve certain endangered species. As he now recalled, after some initial press, word of what was going on with the project had seemed to just die out. Obviously, Jack now realized, that was what the government had wanted.

"Here are the zebra," Pike said, "hang on." He banked and took the helicopter into a shallow dive headed directly for the herd.

As the craft lost altitude and began to close in, the zebra took flight. Pike found one that was running near the edge and singled it out. He dropped in still closer. Jack glanced at the altimeter. They were at a hundred and fifty feet.

As the singled out zebra broke from the herd in a full gallop, Pike took the chopper down to forty feet. "Weincamp settled on the zebra because of it's long distance running capabilities," he said. "And as you can see, if she perceives her survival to be in question she'll continue to run away from us, literally until she drops."

Suddenly the zebra cut left sharply, back toward the herd. "She may be runnin'" Tiller said, "but she sure as shit ain't runnin' straight."

"No, she's not."

"Dog whistle would do a better job."

"With the survival instinct used in its pure form, maybe so, Al. But Weincamp customized it, so to speak. He came up with a process called Inverse Determination."

"Inverse what?" Polling asked.

"Inverse Determination. It works like this. If an animal like this zebra is running from a predator she will continue until she is physically unable to go farther — the point of physical collapse. And that's what Weincamp needed. The direction of her movement, however, is in question, as we've just seen. So Weincamp developed a method which would make Moonmare experience the equivalent of being chased by, say, a starving lion, but her perception of escape from the danger was not to run *away* from it, but rather directly *toward* it. In that way she has no choice. Her path is totally predictable in every case. She will run in a direct line toward what she imagines as her only *escape* route."

He pulled the helicopter up and away from the herd.

"You mean, Moonmare is scared out of her wits constantly?" Jack said. He was starting to feel the repulsion again.

"Yes and no. The survival instinct is continually called into play, but you'll remember when we looked at Moonmare's internal organs there were two brains."

"Right," Jack said. "An emotional one and a logical one, if I remember right."

"Exactly. Well, the emotional brain is what reads the Caller's vibrations as the equivalent of a predator in pursuit. But for purposes of her general consciousness — which, by the way, is also something different than you or I experience — the signal is overridden by her logical brain."

"Meaning?"

"Her fright is suppressed. She doesn't consciously know she's experiencing it."

"Let me get this straight," Jack said. "She's scared out of her wits constantly, but running directly toward what she thinks is the threat, because somehow it appears to be her only *escape*... and she doesn't realize she's afraid?"

"That's exactly it. She's just galloping along up there, sending us information and not really knowing why she keeps on the go."

"Incredible." Jack whispered to himself, shaking his head.

"We ain't goin' up there to catch this pony, are we?" Tiller said.

"Catch her and kill her," Pike said. "And don't ask me anymore about that. You'll get the whole scoop tomorrow from a special guest speaker."

TWENTY-THREE

That evening Jack went back to his room after dinner and turned on the news. There was more talk about the sagging economy, educational deterioration in America and, of course, presidential candidates making promises.

After five minutes of this Jack found himself unable to concentrate. He muted the sound. The first thoughts that came to his mind were of Muriel. He longed desperately to make love to her and be sure she wasn't afraid. Was she okay, he wondered? When he had first left he'd thought she would be. But now he wasn't sure. She had no doubt gotten his note, but had she been able to handle it? Had she understood what his scribbling meant and that he would be back as soon as he possibly could? As fragile as she was, Jack worried now that she might get panicky and feel he had abandoned her. He hoped to God that had not happened, but he was becoming more and more concerned that it might have. He forced this from his mind, telling himself that she was fine and she had realized he had no choice but to accept this opportunity.

Opportunity, he suddenly thought. That word brought other questions to mind. Was this really an opportunity? Should he have jumped at the chance so eagerly? What was it really all about? And how did everything connect? A scientist who commits suicide and kills a priest for no apparent reason? A robot-like gorilla? A horse-like thing running around on the backside of the moon thinking it will die if it even slows down for a second, but at the same time not realizing that? A top secret trip to the moon to kill her? The more Jack thought about it, the more thoughts like "government cover up" and "inhumane treatment" crept into his mind.

Suddenly he saw the face of Martin Balk on television. The Vice President was speaking to a group of women. Jack turned up the sound as he said, "...so our children must be protected. To those who would threaten those children with drugs and guns and the unsafe streets I say, the battle has just gotten underway. We will reclaim our streets. We will encircle our children. We will drive you who threaten their futures straight to hell!"

The roar of applause went up. Jack turned off the TV. He got to his feet, crossed the room and began looking through the internal phone directory. He found the office number for John Pike. After a moment's hesitation he dialed.

"Hello. This is Pike," the voice answered.

"Hello, John. Jack Moore here."

"Hi, Jack. What can I do for you?"

"This may sound crazy, John, but I have to tell you, I have a few reservations about everything I've been hearing over the past few days."

"I see. Well, can I help?"

"I think so. Didn't you know Andrew Weincamp personally?"

"Yes, I did."

"Listen, John, maybe it would do me some good to just talk out some of these questions. Frankly, I feel comfortable sharing these things with you, and I think you just may be the guy with some of the answers. Is there a chance we could meet?"

"Sure. You know where my room is?"

"No, but I'm pretty good at directions."

Ten minutes later Jack got out of an elevator on the fourth floor. He moved left following Pike's directions and headed down a stairway. He moved down a long corridor with only an occasional door and, again per instructions, turned left at a "T" junction.

As he approached the junction, he passed a door left ajar and caught a peek inside as he moved by. He saw what looked like a large hotel linen and wash room. There were stacks of white towels and sheets, clothes hampers, huge sacks and, set into a shallow alcove, what looked like the handset and metal cord of a pay telephone. He briefly wondered if it was restricted like the room phones. As he moved by he thought not. Why have a payphone, he reasoned, if you couldn't call out on it?

Then he rounded another corner and came to a door at the end of the corridor. It was marked with a "5".

It, too, was ajar. He knocked and heard Pike's friendly voice say, "Come on in, Jack."

Jack entered and found a rather large, apartment-like business office in two sections. On the left was a desk, computer, credenza and telephone, all in a small cubicle. It was partitioned off by two chest high dividers. Jack noticed the computer was on and the familiar ASNA Intranet browser was up.

Pike's voice came from the right. "Have a seat, Jack. I'm just finishing off this proposal." He was seated on a couch with a briefcase opened on the coffee table, doing paperwork. Beside the briefcase was a drink. It looked like scotch. At one end of the couch was a bar and, sure enough, set out on it was a bottle of Cutty Sark, glasses, and an ice bucket.

"Want a drink?" Pike asked.

"No, thanks," Jack said. He took a seat in a comfortable easy chair across from the sofa.

Pike finished writing, placed the papers in his briefcase and moved it all off onto the carpet. He took a long pull from the scotch and said, "Okay, so tell me what's on your mind."

"Actually," Jack said, "there's a lot on my mind. But the first thing is Weincamp. Forgive me for being skeptical or suspicious, John, but it just seems odd that a few weeks ago this world renowned scientist, who you now tell us was making incredible genetic breakthroughs, suddenly waltzes into a church, kills a priest, then blows his own brains out."

Pike was nodding.

"And add to that the fact that two weeks later here we all are getting ready to go to the moon and do away with everything he ever worked for? I mean, am I being paranoid here or does there seem to be some connection?"

Pike put the drink down. He had become serious, but he was still his personable self. "I have to tell you," he said, "I had some of the same feelings when I was called into this thing — which wasn't that long before you, by the way. But you're right, I *did* know Weincamp. He was a brilliant man, Jack, but he really wasn't all that stable. He had also developed a severe drinking problem. Did you know that?"

"No."

"And the guy was prone to some weird activities."

"Such as?"

"Such as a few months ago when he showed up drunk or high on something at a college pep rally and sat in on, would you believe, a government protest."

"Did this make the papers?"

"I don't think so. Most people, including the press, didn't realize just how important a man he was. I think they kind of brushed him aside as some radical old fart with a political bone to pick. And his drinking and drug use and all the other crazy business he started getting into was kept pretty quiet. I think he was basically pacified to keep him productive and out of the limelight. So frankly, when I heard what he had done, I was sad — I mean he really was an incredible mind — but I wasn't all that surprised."

Jack felt Pike was being sincere, and what he said seemed to fit in with Weincamp's death. But there was still the question of Moonmare. "So what about this Moonmare. This half zebra, half I'm not sure what? Why suddenly decide to kill her? I mean, you said she was successful. And it seems like after the work Weincamp put in and all the money it cost to get her up there, the powers that be would want to keep her alive."

"That all comes tomorrow. And I'll tell you right up front I know a *little* more than you, but, Jack, I don't have anywhere near all the details myself. And that goes for the Moonmare project in general. I'm going to be listening real close, just like you."

"To who?"

"I'm not supposed to say in advance. Security. But I can tell you this, he's the guy in the know. No question about it."

TWENTY-FOUR

The telephone on the desk between Angie Mays and William Carr emitted a pleasant tone. Seated beside each other in a darkened computer room on the fifth floor of Saltridge, the pair were surrounded by monitors, printers, drives, equipment racks and routing switchers. Mays had been making minor program adjustments to what the scientists referred to as CONCH, the Caller Optimal Network Control Hub. Carr, meanwhile, had been leafing through pages in a "Muscle and Fitness" magazine.

Mays took the call. "CONCH-OP. Mays."

As she listened to the caller, Carr paused turning pages and looked her way. Moments later he heard her confirm an official order and saw her begin to jot down a series of numbers. He knew these would be times, frequency levels and global lunar coordinates. When she had read back and confirmed the numbers, Mays hung up and said, "Okay, Willie, enough of the hard bodies. Time to send our Mare off to new horizons."

Carr chuckled. "Hard bodies. I wish!"

"You're not that much overweight, right? What? Only about 50 pounds or so?"

Both laughed.

"Thanks a lot, Twiggy," Carr said. "What's the deal?"

"An immediate course correction. Let's see…" As she said this, Mays tapped and brought up a graphic on the master screen headed with the words *"Caller Network – Data/Loc Overview"*. Beneath it were a column of numbers, at the lower right a single bar graph, and in the upper right corner, a spiderweb-like network of Caller locations superimposed on a graphic of the lunar surface. For each location a point of blue light punctuated spots along the web's outer rim. One was blinking. "…a 22 point 6 degree change to lunar north-north-west," Mays continued.

Carr had brought up the same screen, and, as Mays then read off a series of numbers, he sequenced through a list of Caller longitude and latitude coordinates along with their potential frequency ranges and surrounding geographical data. Moments later he arrived at a point on his lunar map. "Ah, Caller 11!" he said.

"That's it. I wonder what's up now?"

"Isn't that at the abandoned observation tower at the west edge of Moscoviense?"

"Right again. Ready for Freq and Amp levels?"

"Ready."

As she then began to read off a second series of numbers, Carr input them and double checked them for errors. When both he and Mays were satisfied the values were correct, Mays picked up the phone and punched in a number. After a moment she said, "Yes, sir. C-5. Mays here, Confirming deactivation of Caller 4 and immediate activation of Caller 11. Values and coordinates as follows…"

When she had completed reading the numbers, she waited for several moments. Then, after receiving a final confirmation, she hung up the phone and turned to Carr. "We're good to go," she said.

"And we're off," Carr said as he started the change activation sequence. After the final click of his mouse, he sat back and smiled.

The darkness changed.

She was not sure how, but it was a change that had happened before. A good change — at least for a short time. One part of her entity weakened.

Though she would not have been able to define or even begin to understand this process of diminishing influence, she was able to experience and sense it. The fright began to fade. Her reason for continued effort and exhaustion was slowly being swept away.

Another part of her was drawing strength from this difference. A transfer of power was taking place. What had increased was the need — the part of her that felt she should not be alone, the part that insisted there should be some touch or sight or spiritual connection with another being. This part of her was also troubled because she sensed that need would not be satis-

fied. Troubled or not, however, simply needing was a great relief from the normal unrelenting sense of horror that was the most powerful force in her existence.

The change continued, and as the horror faded her reason to move ahead faded with it. Her exhaustion continued to diminish also.

She was slowing down.

And then the movement was gone. A great physical strain was instantly removed from her tremendous body. The grueling labor of having to lift her giant legs and hooves had left her.

She was standing still.

It was daylight on the backside of the moon and surrounding her was a blaze of white light — a hot, reflective plane stretching in all directions to seeming infinity.

Some basic instinct told her to describe the expanse before her. She tried but that was no longer possible. She'd had that power once, but it had long ago been garbled inside her by the fright and turned into a random stream of meaningless pleadings — an endless, horrific, outpouring of digital nonsense. She saw, but the mathematical descriptions of those images simply would not articulate.

What did make sense at this moment, were groups of sensory feelings generated by the parts of her existence. The glimmer of hope was growing into a spark.

The need was intensifying.

The fright had totally gone.

There was no pursuit and no fear of annihilation, just the light and loneliness and a great intense heat.

Then, suddenly, it started to return.

In the ground beneath her the fear rose up slowly at first. It grew quickly and began to dominate the other parts of her with its paralyzing grasp.

Her body shook with repulsion. She swung around toward the fear. She reared up on her thick hind legs and found a new place on the horizon. As she began to move the exhaustion poured back into her weary body. The hope dwindled again to only a glimmer and the need was simply dominated and squelched by the horror that was now filling every part of her.

She was alone and running.

But things were different.

Though she didn't yet realize it, she was now on a course that would provide the answers she sought.

TWENTY-FIVE

The nightmare came again — this time worse.

And this time Jack was in it. At first he was behind her, holding her head in place so she couldn't turn away from the light. She could feel his large, warm fingers pressing on her cheeks and temples. And from behind her his voice kept blaring. He was laughing, saying, "Go for it, kid. Just fucking go for it."

She struggled to turn over but couldn't. She was held in place by his hands and the sickening weight of some horrible presence. And when she tried to talk to Jack, to plead with him, what came out of her mouth weren't words, but the squeals of a baby.

Then, as always, the liquid fell onto her face, the stale yeasty droplets. The light became more intense. It flared out from behind the silhouette of a man's head above her. She continued to try to plead, but to no avail. And all the while Jack was behind her, laughing.

Then a face was there, a stranger's face. He was turning away, saying something crazy about the freezer.

For a moment, for just an instant, he turned back and their eyes met. She saw a deep, horrible fear in them, and she knew she was looking into the eyes of a man about to commit murder.

"Go for it, kid," Jack continued. "It's no big deal!" And now his hands clamped down even tighter on the sides of her face. They began to squeeze hard and again she tried to talk, but the only sounds she could hear were squeals.

Suddenly she knew they were the screams of a child when it's being born — when its head is in the grip of the forceps.

The stranger – no the *doctor* — looked directly into her eyes and his face was red and swollen and it seemed as if he were about to cry.

Her jaw felt as if it would cave in from the pressure of Jack's hands — the forceps. Then he began to pull and her neck began to stretch and pop inside. Her skull was going to separate from her spine. She could feel the bones and cartilage straining to hold together. She was screaming, choking, and suddenly Jack began laughing. The doctor tuned away crying out loud.

She screamed and...came awake.

In the moments that followed Muriel didn't think at all about what she was doing. She clicked on the light still gasping for air. She reached for the phone and dialed Jack's number. She had to speak to him. She had to tell him and it had to be now.

His machine answered. "Hello, this is Jack Moore. I'm not in at the moment, but —" She slammed down the phone, picked it up again and redialed — this time his number at the base.

She was surprised when a friendly male voice answered. "Hello, Lieutenant Colonel Moore's office, this is Captain Artolus. May I help you?"

The voice forced her to pause and partly regain her composure. She stuttered, trembled and caught her breath. "Ah, y...yes. Yes, I'd-like to...to speak with, ah, Lieutenant Colonel Moore, please." As she said this she forced herself to relax her constricted throat, praying, hoping with all of her being that the person on the other end would say, "Just a minute please, he's right here, ma'am."

Her heart sank when instead he said what she had really expected, "I'm sorry ma'am, but Lieutenant Colonel Moore is not in. Can I or someone else help you?"

She was trying with every ounce of will she had not to sound panicked, but it was no use. Her voice quavered uncontrollably and she kept losing her breath. "Well...I...I just need to...talk with him...1 just...Oh, God, do you know where he is?"

"Ma'am is everything all right?"

Calm down, she told herself. *Damn it, get hold of yourself, you neurotic little bitch! Just stop it!* "Yes...yes, I'm, I'm okay. I'm, well, I'm just a good friend of his. I mean, we're...going to be...married and... well, is there, is there any way I can reach him? Just talk to him for...for a second, or something?... Please?"

There was a long silence on the other end. Finally the voice came back. "Hang on just a second, ma'am."

Again her hopes soared. Was it possible they could reach him? Was he close by? Just walking in the room? Running to get to the phone and talk to her? Would he be mad at her for calling? Would he hate her? God! What would he —"

"General Mathias, may I help you?"

Oh my God, she thought. *A General!* She was going to ruin Jack's career. *Get a hold on yourself Goddamnit! Stop this stupidity! Just calm your ass down!* "Ah, yes," she said, "I had just, ah, I had just hoped to speak with, ah, Lieutenant Colonel Moore."

"Are you…related to Jack, ma'am?" the voice came back, kindly.

"No, I'm not. Not yet. I, well, I'm a good friend of his and —"

"Ma'am, Lieutenant Colonel Moore is on special assignment. I expect him back in his office in approximately three weeks. If this is not a family matter or a life or death emergency, I'd like to hold your message until that time."

Life or death! Yes, absolutely! Tell him it's an emergency, she thought. *Just go ahead! Tell him you're dying! Say: "General, you bet your fucking brass this is an emergency! I am losing my Goddamned mind! Do you understand me? And I can't stop it!"*

"Ma'am, may I have your name, please."

"Ah, yes, Olsen. Muriel Olsen." She suddenly got hold of herself. "And…my message can wait. I don't want to disturb him."

"Can I ask what your relationship is to Lieutenant Colonel Moore, ma'am?"

With those words, with that polite, concerned question a new kind of fear suddenly surfaced in Muriel's mind. She became frightened of this man. The tone in his voice seemed to have changed slightly. It was composed and gentle enough, but somehow it suddenly seemed to be probing. Was it really? Was there a sinister ring to it? Was Jack in trouble? Or was she just imagining it? She got a split second mental image of a cruel, pockmarked face on the other end of the line. "Well, I'm his friend. I'm a good friend of his," she said, "but I —"

"And are you calling locally, ma'am, or long distance?"

She realized she had to hang up and quickly. "Ah, local. But I'll just call back another time. I realize he's busy... And we can always talk later. Thank you for all your trouble. Really."

"Ma'am, I'd like to know —"

"I'm so sorry. I really have to go now."

She slammed the phone down, unsure of what she had just done, or what she should do next.

She looked out her window.

The moon was full.

She leaped from her bed and ran toward the shower.

TWENTY-SIX

The next morning when Jack looked out his window, he noticed a helicopter on what had previously been a vacant chopper pad on a small knoll just south of his building. A black, unmarked SUV had parked close by, and adjacent to it, on a lawn area near a stand of olive trees, he saw a Mercedes Benz. Another SUV had pulled onto a nearby ridge in the distance. Two men in suits chatted on the sidewalk below.

Jack showered, shaved, and headed for breakfast. He ran into Tiller and Polling. As Jack took a seat, Polling had just stuck her spoon into a half cantaloupe, saying to Tiller, "I'm sure he was the head of the ASNA not that long ago."

Tiller picked up on the thought as he slurped a mouth full of sausage and syrupy hot cakes. "Yeah, he was. And he was a pilot, too. Hell of a guy. Loves his country. I bet it is him."

"Who?" Jack asked.

"Martin Balk," Tiller said. "The Vice President. We think he's the speaker today."

Somehow Jack felt immediately that Tiller was right. Of course, he thought. It would fit with everything else perfectly. He had seen Balk on TV many times recently and the politician seemed to fit the rest of the pattern of this whole series of events. He had been associated with the ASNA, so he must have worked closely with Weincamp at some point. And there was something about him that, for Jack, just didn't seem quite right. He was too smooth, too perfect. When asked about important issues, he seemed to be a master at pouring forth an abundance of official, eloquent sounding rhetoric that lacked any real substance or specifics.

Jack was handed a menu by a young male server. He ordered a fruit cup, cottage cheese, toast and coffee.

Forty minutes later Pike stood at the head of the conference room introducing Balk. "We've covered a lot since the three of you arrived," he said. "Some of the information has been easy enough to accept and I know some has been a little tough to swallow. And I know you all have important questions. I've been avoiding some of them for a good reason. I didn't want to give half accurate answers or get into assumptions. You should all know exactly what the facts are, why they're so urgent, and why what you're about to do is so important to this country. To give you those facts I'd like to introduce a man we all admire very much, and the person I've got my money on as the next President of the United States. Vice President Martin Balk."

Balk stood up and Jack was amazed at how tall he was in person. Six-three or four, Jack thought. Every hair on his head was perfectly in place, slicked straight back. His pinstriped navy blue suit jacket was buttoned and his collar was heavily starched, framing a bright, gun metal gray, silk tie. He was calm and intelligent looking with a large forehead, slightly pock-marked skin and piercing hazel eyes.

"Good morning," he said with a warm, comfortable smile. "Let me be sure I've got it right, here." He pointed at Tiller. "Colonel Allan Tiller, pilot, commander, recipient of two Hostile Action Awards and a Purple Heart?"

Tiller beamed with pride. He stood and saluted. "At your command, sir."

Balk nodded, pleased, and said, "Thank you for your service, Colonel. Then he looked at Jack, "And Lieutenant Colonel Jack Moore, also a combat veteran and tcst pilot."

Jack stood, saluted and said, "Yes, sir."

He received no nod from Balk. Perhaps because he wasn't decorated like Tiller.

"And finally," Balk continued, "Captain Janice Polling, recently back from Afghanistan."

Polling stood up and saluted much like Tiller had done and said, "Yes, sir. Pleased to meet you Mister Vice President, sir, and proud to be of service."

Balk smiled. "Thank you, captain," he said. "I appreciate that, but more importantly, your country appreciates it."

Again Tiller and Polling beamed.

Balk glanced at Jack briefly, then began. "Well, I won't waste time on old news. You are all well aware of what we're calling Operation Roundup and what your basic mission is. What I'd like to do today is give you the 'whys' behind a lot of what you've been hearing.

"Let me start with what I consider one of the most important aspects of this whole business and that's Doctor Andrew Weincamp. Andrew was a personal friend of mine and a brilliant man. I worked closely with him over nearly a twenty year development period during project Moonmare, and I want to make it clear up front that I had enormous respect for the man, both as a scientist and a friend. Weincamp has literally changed the course of genetic science. Without going into more detail on his death because, I'll be perfectly frank, I find it painful, still, let me just say it was a great shock to me and all members of the circle of his close friends. Let me add that it was also an incalculable setback to his field of study."

Jack glanced around the room. All eyes were intent on this man. He was brilliant, and in full control.

He paused, seeming to gather his thoughts and shift focus. "In a personal sense," he continued, "the majority of Weincamp's life work was Moonmare. In a much broader sense it was to give man the ability to explore and eventually even colonize the farthest and most hostile regions of space. When you really look at the facts, Drew Weincamp opened the door to the universe for us. Had Moonmare been a complete success we might be stepping though that door today. As it turns out, the door is left ajar at this point and we are now able to peer through it. And while we see fantastic opportunities beyond its threshold, we also see that there are barriers to be overcome."

Jack spoke impulsively. "Of which Moonmare has become one?"

Balk paused. For just an instant he seemed to be irritated by the interruption, but then his smooth, controlled manner returned. "Yes, Jack. Unfortunately, that's right. And since that's probably the issue uppermost in all of your minds, let's get straight to it.

"The research time, resources, and logistics involved in the development of Moonmare were astronomical to say the least. It took literally half a lifetime of personal genetic work and nearly a decade of preparation, both on the moon and here on earth. In the course of this research, Weincamp attempted to cover every base. And when you consider how many bases there were, you begin to realize how incredibly successful he was."

Come on, Jack thought to himself, *cut the political bullshit and get to the point.*

"Unfortunately, however, he overlooked one critical aspect of his creation..."

Finally, Jack thought.

"...her growth." Balk removed a notecard from his breast pocket. "According to Weincamp's calculations, Moonmare was not supposed to grow at all. She was "born", so to speak, full size. At that point her dimensions were," he looked down at the card, "weight, eighteen-hundred pounds, height, six feet at the shoulder, length eleven feet nose to rump. Her physical size was roughly that of a very large, overweight zebra."

Tiller looked unimpressed.

Balk paused and leveled his gaze at each of the astronauts. "One month later," he continued, "weight, twenty-four hundred pounds, height at the shoulder, eight feet, overall length, sixteen feet."

Polling's eyes opened wide.

"The following month," Balk continued, "weight, four *thousand*, five-hundred pounds...height, approximately thirteen feet at the shoulder, length, just over nineteen feet."

"Jesus." Tiller exclaimed. "This ain't no little filly!"

"More like a dinosaur!" Polling added.

"You're both getting the idea. In fact, today we estimate her at, now get ready here, approximate weight, thirty-thousand, three-hundred pounds. Height at the shoulder, forty-two feet and length, nose to rump, fifty-nine feet."

Pike looked around the table. The group appeared in shock trying to imagine the size of such a creature. He added, "So you can see, what we've got going on here is some sort of chain reaction. At least that's what we think."

Polling said, "Won't it eventually stop?"

"We're not sure," Balk said, "and before that happens, if it does, we've got some major problems."

"For instance," Jack asked.

"For instance, she is even now actually creating very small tremors on the moon detectable by sensitive equipment here on earth. These are movements which we're aware of, of course, but we'rc fairly confident that in the near future other countries will begin to pick them up as something other than natural ground movements."

"The galloping," Jack said, "rhythmic, repetitive vibrations that can only be made by something mechanical or alive."

"Exactly."

"Why not just cut the signal or umbilical, or whatever it is, and drop her in her tracks right now?" Tiller asked.

"We could do that, Al, certainly, but that creates other problems. First, there has been increased talk in the world community of exploration and even possible colonization of the moon. Moonmare is a top secret organism. We don't want to simply leave her lying around for some other country to eventually discover.

"In addition, Doctor Weincamp was, and the council of individuals who have overseen the Moonmare project from its inception still are, convinced that with flesh and organ samples of Moonmare in our hands we can find out what caused her growth disorder and correct it on future projects."

"Which is where we come in," Jack said.

"Exactly," Balk said, and again he seemed to glare at Jack for an instant. "We've decided we needed a team of the best possible astronauts we could find to get up there and take care of this business. You three were picked. You're all top notch in your field, you all have top secret clearances, you're all unattached and you're all distinguished military veterans."

"Unattached?" Jack said.

"Right, Jack. With a mission this secret and, to be frank, this dangerous, well, it's just a lot less... complicated I guess, to have no wife and kids back home."

"I see," Jack said. He noticed Balk looking closely at him. There seemed to be an awkward silence.

Tiller broke it. "So how do we get this job done?" he asked with relish, "And when do we leave?"

Balk liked this response. He smiled. "That," he said, "you are about to find out. I'm off to a meeting this afternoon, but John will take over from here with those details."

He paused again, dramatically. Jack knew what was coming. More patriotic bullshit.

"And with that, let me just say that I am extremely proud to have met each of you personally. I look forward to meeting again with you right after your return." He stopped and smiled. "In fact, since the world will never know what you've done, the President and I have a private get-together set up for you. A little coming home medal celebration, you might say."

This last comment made Tiller and Polling both squirm in their seats with excitement. It was a perfect carrot, Jack thought. They would take this mission on brimming over with patriotism and hell bent on accomplishing it at all costs.

Jack was envisioning Muriel. *Unattached.... No wife and kids back home.* He suddenly felt even more worried for her than he had the night before.

Later that morning Jack ate lunch by himself. He tried to read a newspaper, but found he couldn't shake two main fears.

First, he was suddenly very concerned about Muriel's well being and he wasn't quite sure why. It hadn't been that long since he had seen her, but it seemed like ages. He was now becoming convinced he shouldn't have left so abruptly. In fact, he was becoming convinced he should have simply said no to the mission and gone forward with their plans.

Then there was Moonmare. Jack had the constant, nagging feeling, whenever that name came up, that some terrible inhumanity had been done to her. He couldn't exactly say what or why, but it had to do with the basic ideology of what she was. Granted, she wasn't really an animal organism in any way, but it seemed she was conscious and had feelings.

Pike talked of this so-called logical brain of hers overriding the fear of death. Even so, did she still have some understanding of what death meant? If not, why did she keep running? Was she conscious like a human being? Aware of her surroundings? And, God, her size! How huge she must be. Since the moon's gravitational force was only one sixth that of earth's, however, it made sense that an organism of that size could continue to run for long periods of time. But even in a reduced gravitational environment he had trouble imagining her existing.

And just how would they do away with her, he wondered? How do you kill something the size of a Tyrannosaurus Rex? He dropped the paper, took a bite of his salad and anticipated what he might be told that afternoon.

TWENTY-SEVEN

The drive from Muriel's apartment to her mother's grave in Ventura County took nearly four hours.

She had gotten on the road less than thirty minutes after waking from the nightmare, allowing herself just enough time to shower, dress, and brush her teeth. As she did these things she kept repeating to herself, "It's going to be okay now. You've made the decision. That was the hard part and now it's over. It's going to be okay. You've decided and you've done the right thing."

These words both consoled and occupied her mind until she climbed into her Honda Civic, fastened the seatbelt, and started the engine. Seconds later she pulled out of the apartment complex under a shroud of stars and darkness.

The time was 4:47 A.M.

For the first two hours the drive was easy. In the desert it was dark and windy and the blackness smelled of sage and tamarisk. The freeway snaked up out of the western Coachella Valley, the dry sand basin only twenty feet above sea level in which the town of La Quinta lay. It climbed to an elevation of nearly two thousand feet at the cities of Cabazon and Banning.

By six o'clock the sun was coming up and she had left the desert. As she moved through the cities of Duarte and Monrovia traffic began to thicken. Half an hour later she found herself in Burbank, immersed in the stop and go bumper-to-bumper traffic bound for Los Angeles. When her mind began to doubt her decision and tempt her to turn back, she bore down, talked out loud to herself and kept her focus. She was close and she had made the decision. It was going to be okay now.

Forty minutes later she passed north of the city of Los Angeles and traffic lightened again. At 8:20 a.m. she parked her car in the small tar parking lot at Simpson Brother's Cemetery, in Thousand Oaks.

She walked into the office and found a young girl by herself. She had evidently just opened and was starting a pot of coffee in a small waiting area. "Hi. Can I help you?" she said, with a youthful, bubbly smile.

"Yes," Muriel said trying to appear calm and emotionless. "I'd like to visit the grave of Sandra Olsen, please." The girl took the request as if Muriel had asked for two lumps of sugar instead of one. "Sure thing," she said, moving to the main desk.

She sat and keyed the name into her computer. "Section 4B," she said a moment later. "Past the office, then left. Go to your first right and stop at the oak tree. It's on your left."

"Thank you."

"Oh, sure. You're welcome… Coffee?"

"No, thank you," Muriel said, stepping out of the office. Several minutes later she parked her car at section 4B. She took a deep breath and again told herself this was the right thing — the only thing — to do. She got out and walked to her mother's grave. Arriving at the two foot square granite plate she looked over the name and dates: Sandra Anne Olsen, 1946 - 2007. She knelt and prayed and this brought her back to the day her mother had died.

———

She had gotten the call from her Uncle John — her mother's older brother. His voice had trembled as he spoke. "Mur, honey, it's your Ma. She's…a stroke, we think. She's slipping, Mur. For Christ sakes, we're not sure she knows us, but she's asking for *you*. Will you come? We're losing her. Can you come now, hon?"

"Is Dad there?" Muriel had asked.

"Yeah. Sure he is, but—"

"I can't."

"Honey, this is your mother we're talking about!"

The words were the most difficult Muriel would ever speak.

"I'm sorry."

"But Mur, sweetie. Honey, she *needs* you now!"

"Tell her I love her…and I'm sorry. I can't explain."

It was then that John had gotten furious. "What?" he'd snapped with that outraged German inflection in his voice. "You love her? You love your mother, for

Christ-sakes, and you won't come and hold her hand on the day she dies? What the hell is this? Don't you—"

"Uncle John, you don't understand."

"I do understand."

"No. You don't."

"I understand that you're mad at your father. I know that. He knows. We all know that, honey. So you two don't get along. So you had some problems. But Mur, this is your Goddamned *flesh and blood* — the woman that brought you into this world — and she's slipping away from us, calling out for you. You hear me? And her own daughter won't come and say goodbye? Good God!"

Even now, years later, Muriel felt the same horrible sinking feeling that had swept through her as she had said those words — the selfishness and shame and horrible, inexplicable guilt.

"Uncle John, I can't...I...I just *can't.*"

"Rot in hell, you bitch!" he had hollered, and slammed down the receiver.

Muriel had cried for hours, recalling every beloved thought and emotion she had felt for her mother during the years since she had been gone. Then, on that day, when the crying was done, she had simply gotten into her car and driven aimlessly for hours along the coast.

That had been four years ago.

On this day, she spoke to the grave plate.

"Mom," she said quietly, "I've always loved you with all my heart. And I've...missed you. You have no idea how I've missed you. But you never could have imagined, and there was no way I could have told you...faced you. I...I just couldn't do it ...I...please, Mom, understand me. Please hear me today, and remember how much I love you."

She prayed quietly for fifteen more minutes and felt better — stronger.

She got to her feet and walked back to her car.

It was just past 9:00 A.M.

One more stop.

TWENTY-EIGHT

When Jack entered the conference room after lunch, Pike had a high magnification still image of a lunar area showing on the screen. Superimposed lettering had been added. At the top center its main title was shown in bold red letters: "The North Forty". It was the place the men would go to kill Moonmare.

Jack saw a ninety-acre oval area with a number of special geographical and man-made structures on it. A crater rim at the edge of the larger lunar sea known as Mare Moscoviense bordered the right end. Caller Number 11 stood at the other end of the oval.

Jack also noted a long runway like area labeled "The Chute". It lead away from the rim of the crater directly toward Caller 11, into what appeared to be a smaller crater roughly a hundred meters in diameter. This crater was near the center of the oval and it was labeled "Corral". There were several small, man-made structures on the sight, and what looked like two buildings adjacent to the small center crater. One was labeled "Bunkhouse" and the other, the "Barn".

Pike used the image to give the men an overview of their mission. First, he said, they would undergo specific mission objectives training for several more weeks. They would then launch aboard a Ganymede 11 booster rocket topped by their lunar command module, mission named Pinto.

They would circle the earth three times in orbit adjustment maneuvers, slingshot into space, and make the three day, 240,000 mile trip to the moon. Once there, they would establish a low altitude orbit and Jack and Tiller would descend one day later to the surface. Polling would remain in orbit in Pinto.

Jack and Tiller, Pike said, would work at The North Forty. He also said that Caller 11 had been activated and Moonmare was now on a course across Mare Moscoviense, heading directly toward it.

Her speed was currently seventeen kilometers per hour, he said. Just before reaching the North Forty her course would take her up the long, gentle slope which was actually the inside rim of the crater.

When she crested the rim she would barely be moving as she entered the North Forty. She would then follow the Chute, still on a direct line with Caller 11. This course would bring her downhill into the Corral, which was directly in front of the structure called the Barn.

It was in the Barn that Jack and Tiller would be waiting.

"The critical spot," Pike said, pointing at the image, "is here, when she comes over the crater rim into the Chute. At that point we'll have about thirty seconds. She'll head straight down this way and into the Corral. When she gets in here, two things have to happen, pronto. We'll cut the umbilical and you, Al, fire off a number of charges that you and Jack have set out the day before."

"Why the charges?" Jack asked. "Won't she die when the umbilical is cut?"

"Yes, but not instantly. First, it's just going to stun the hell out of her. The truth is, we don't know exactly how she'll react. And, frankly, we don't want to be taking any chances at all. We want to stop her on the *spot*. Boom. No questions asked. You and Al will only be about fifty yards from her at that point, right over here." He pointed at the Barn.

"You'll be sitting up in the Barn, looking her straight in the eyeballs."

"Up?" Tiller said.

"Yeah, about thirty feet up. Like I said, this was an observation point. It's actually a tower."

"At thirty feet we won't be looking her in the eyes," Jack said, "we'll be looking *up* at her."

"True, but remember, she's fifty yards away, and that's as close as she ever gets. You guys take her out fast, then you get on down in the Buggy there and get your samples. Meanwhile, Janice is overhead in orbit documenting with stills and live video. You two climb back into orbit, come around three times, and head back for earth. When all three of you are safely out of the way... we nuke what's left of her."

"Nuke?" Jack exclaimed. "A nuclear *bomb*?"

"It's the only way to be absolutely sure she and the North Forty are totally destroyed."

"Jesus," Polling said, "vaporized is a better word."

"And just how does this nuclear bomb get up there?" Jack asked.

"It's one of the items you guys set out in advance. It's smaller than you think, actually, and perfectly safe. It can only be armed and detonated by Mission Control back here on earth, and that happens *after* you guys are back in orbit. As far as you're concerned, it's just another suitcase."

"Ain't nobody gonna know this bomb went off back here on earth?" Tiller asked.

"Actually, they may know something went off, but we plan to go with a public announcement that we believe it was a meteor impact. We figure the rest of the world should go along with that."

TWENTY-NINE

At the same meeting, the group was introduced to Air Force Captain Bill Ericson, the Control Engineer who would be the astronauts' single point of contact throughout the mission. Ericson was a muscular, pale-skinned Swede with red hair and a drawn but healthy, freckled face. His handsome, boyish looks were deceiving. He was forty-seven years old, an accomplished IT and aerospace engineer, and a fiercely patriotic military lifer.

As Pike covered each of the events that would soon take place, in many cases Ericson added what his involvement would entail while monitoring the entire mission from the control room. The knowledge and decisiveness he displayed instilled a strong sense of confidence in the group.

Jack liked the engineer the moment they met. They talked the next morning during a pre-dawn jogging session and discovered that they were both astronomy aficionados and Ericson lived just off Baron Air Base, only a few blocks from Jack. When the two had finished their run, they cooled down with some stretches just off the trail. Jack attempted to feel Ericson out. "I'm sure you're great at what you do, Bill, but you can't be the only guy running this show."

"Not by a long shot," Ericson said. "Like John has said, there's a full group that have been a part of the project all along. But I'll be your single point of contact."

"Is there a reason for that? I mean, the rest of the crew knows what this is all about, right?"

"Sure. Well…sort of. But the mission commanders wanted a simple command and control arrangement. I've got plenty of support and high-level back up if I need it, but I'll be the voice of it all as far as you guys are concerned."

"Mission commanders? Who are they? Martin Balk, I guess for one."

"Sorry, Jack. No names. Strict orders. This whole thing really has a lid on it."

"That's for sure."

Deciding he could prod a little more Jack said, "It's kind of strange, you know, this…half zebra, half…whatever up there running around, and Weincamp…" He looked for some indication in Ericson's demeanor that the engineer agreed with him. He saw none.

"I don't question it." Ericson said. "I figure I've got a job to do for this country, and that may sound corny, but I take it real seriously."

"It doesn't sound corny at all. It sounds admirable."

Ericson smiled, obviously proud. "Thanks."

"I'm the same way. I just wonder sometimes about all the things we don't know. Especially with a mission as secret as this. Guess I'm too damn curious."

"Don't get me wrong. I am too. But I place my trust in the guys upstairs. If they say it's right for America, I'm good with that."

"Yeah, me too."

The morning sun had just cleared the horizon. The desert smelled fresh and wild. The sand was awash with reddish light and long shadows. Jack and Ericson moved from the jogging trail toward the gym entrance. "Well, I've got no doubt we'll be in good hands up there," Jack said.

"Thanks. You guys can count on me."

"I know we can."

THIRTY

Martin Balk landed at his west coast beach house just over an hour after leaving the group at Saltridge. The house was a sprawling, tile roofed, Spanish style home set comfortably into the rolling hills above Malibu, California. Its low plaster arches and lush fern planters were accented by a colorful tile-trimmed fountain in the center of a circular driveway. Several acres of scrub oak and eucalyptus were spread over the gentle brown hills covering the seventeen acres which surrounded it.

Immediately after the helicopter had set down on the helipad at the rear of the house, Balk insisted on complete privacy. He went straight to his study. He poured a Grey Goose, La Vanille vodka on ice and spent several minutes at the large bay window that faced out toward the ocean. "Opportunities," he said out loud. It was incredible how some potential problems seemed to just pop right into the open as if asking to be taken care of in advance. "Muriel Olsen," he whispered with a smile. "Sweet Muriel Olsen..."

He removed his jacket, rolled up his sleeves, and moved to his desk. He took a seat and loosened his tie. He opened his briefcase and removed a file with Muriel's name on it. He began to leaf through the more than twenty pages of pictures and information it contained. As he did he shook his head and chuckled. Half an hour later, as he was still going through the material, the phone rang.

"Balk," he said.

"Miller here."

"Where are you?"

"Santa Barbara. About five hours drive from the desert."

"Is she busy?"

"For the moment. Not sure for how long."

"Doing what?"

"She just went into a nut house."

THIRTY-ONE

When viewed from Highway 101 in Santa Barbara, the Oakview Psychiatric Hospital looks like a moderate-sized estate set into distant rolling hills dotted with oak, palm and eucalyptus trees. Once Muriel had gotten off the highway, however, and driven up to the front of the hospital, she realized it was much larger.

Its low, ranch-style architecture consistcd of nearly a dozen diagonal rows of tile roofed, single story buildings. These were bordered by stands of pepper trees, groups of palms, and wide lawn areas which reminded Muriel of a small golf course. The entire area stretched back into a long, shallow valley set between two grassy hills.

As she approached the hospital she saw a small sign above what she assumed was the administrative office entrance. It read, simply, "Oakview Psychiatric Hospital."

Muriel parked and, again, concentrated on focusing her thoughts. "This is it," she whispered to herself. "It's the right thing — the last thing. Don't think. Don't question. Don't chicken out. Just go!"

She got out of her car, walked in the front door, and told the fat, elderly receptionist she wanted to see her father, Gunter Olsen. After several quizzical looks and a check of her I.D., the receptionist left the office. Moments later a manager approached.

"Forgive us, Ms. Olsen," the woman said kindly. "But we've had Gunter here for nearly three years now and…"

"And I've never visited."

"Well…yes."

"I haven't been able to, until now. It's just become possible."

The woman stared at Muriel for what seemed like a long, awkward moment, as if she were looking for some indication of a lie. Finally she spoke again. "Are you aware of your father's mental state at this point?"

"No."

"I'm afraid he's unable to communicate."

Muriel's throat constricted immediately. She wheezed slightly as she said, "…Comatose?"

"Yes, I'm afraid so."

Muriel felt herself hyperventilating. She forced it back. "I see," she said. "For how long?"

"Over a year now."

Muriel was on the verge of turning around and leaving. Could she possibly go through with this? What good would it do to see him now? No. That was an excuse — her weak, guilt ridden mind saying, *Just give up, Muriel. Just go back. You can't bear to see him. Just go and live with your sickness. Just settle for being a basket case. Jack will understand. Sure he will.*

But she held her resolve. It *would* do good. It would free her. It was a trip she would never find the strength to make again. "I understand," she finally said to the manager. "I'd just like to spend a few minutes with him, if that's okay."

Again, for just a moment the woman seemed to ponder Muriel's request with suspicion. Then she picked up the phone and called for a nurse. Seconds later a tiny, dwarflike Hispanic woman in a white dress appeared.

"Elba," the manager said, "take Ms. Olsen to twenty one."

They walked down a long, quiet corridor lined with doors. At the end was a huge window. It bathed the smooth linoleum floor in a wash of blinding white light.

Muriel was trembling with anxiety. She kept expecting to hear horrific voices or see drooling, demented people dart out from corners and shadows, but there were none — just the stillness and the blaze of light off the linoleum floor.

They turned a corner and came to room twenty-one.

The nurse opened the door and Muriel stepped in.

He was lying in a bed that had been adjusted up into a nearly sitting position. His bed was beside a window. He looked as if he were simply relaxing and staring out into the dry grassy hills.

There was a chair by the bed.

Muriel approached and sat beside him.

She was amazed at how he had changed. When she'd last seen him he had been heavy and brown, with a tough, leathery face and a full beard. Now he was pale, milky, and extremely thin. He had become bald and his face was pock marked, sunken and dry looking. He looked clean, amazingly clean and white, she thought, and peaceful.

It was as if someone had scrubbed all the cigar smoke and beer and evil out of his mind and body. As if they had found a way to cleanse his soul and then simply set him down for an afternoon to enjoy his new found purity.

He blinked occasionally, but gave no other indication he was aware of her presence.

Her mind went back over the years.

Oddly, she first remembered the good times — the slides in the parks, the beaches and hot dogs, picnics and country rides. She recalled the theme parks and fairs and the late night summer trips to Anderson's ice cream shop. She remembered his smile, loving and happy, and the way he had thrown her into the air squealing and caught her with such ease. She remembered evenings by the TV, and mornings in the breakfast nook, and eventually these lead to the nightmare.

He had changed slowly, she remembered, just as she had changed. They had gone through a kind of tense, grotesque, metamorphosis together. As she had begun to mature into a woman, he'd lost several jobs in a row and started drinking heavily. And the way they touched each other became different. The grip when he held her arm was no longer a kid grip — no longer a firm, loving father's hold. There was something odd in it she remembered — a strange, uncomfortable gentleness that was magnified by his increased drinking and smoking.

She sensed the difference in his touch only slightly at first, and for a long time she thought little of it. Then he began to talk differently to her also. It was no longer, "Hey there, kiddo, what's up?" in the gruff, jovial voice of her father. Instead it became softer, gentler, and often slurred.

"How are you, Muriel? Feeling good today, hon?" he would say.

At the same time his eyes, too, began to change. They became bloodshot and their sky blue orbs slowly became sullen and dark. As that humid summer of emerging womanhood had come on, she remembered his eyes had seemed almost to glaze over with shadows of irrational tenderness...desire.

"Hot as hell, isn't it, Mur, honey," he would say, wiping his chest with a handkerchief. "Like a damn sauna bath!"

All this had created a kind of unspoken discomfort between them, a subtle shroud of fear and repulsion.

"So humid and...steamy, Mur, baby...Jesus."

Though she had her suspicions, she hadn't been completely sure of what all this meant until that oven-like, summer night of the party.

Her mother had flown to New York on a week long visit with relatives. Muriel, now eighteen, had gone to a keg party — one of the few she had ever attended.

And for some reason she had drunk heavily. The wine coolers had gone down amazingly easy and she remembered thinking she had never realized how simple it was to drink and loose all inhibitions and totally free her mind. But before the night was over, the drinking had gone far beyond that stage.

Her friends had dropped her off at 2 A.M. in a stupor on her front porch. They had rung the bell and run to their car and he had come to the door. He'd been drunk, too, as had often been the case in those years.

She'd been too far gone to realize what was happening. When he first picked her up she thought he must be carrying her to her bed, and when she'd fallen onto the mattress at first she thought she had been right. Then, someplace, mixed in with the dizziness and confusion, she'd realized it wasn't her bed.

"So damned hot...clothes just...stick to your...oh, Christ, your body, Mur, hon...."

The dark room had spun with the moon blazing white through the window behind his head. He was a silhouette. His eyes were barely visible, but there was something terrible in them.

"God, baby, so fucking...hot!"

The light behind his head — the full moon — was blinding. She was becoming sick as the room spun and the sweat from his face was falling on her chest and neck. He was moving on top of her and pulling at her underwear as the drops of hot, smoky sweat came down, burning into her eyes and flesh, coating her in the smell of stale beer and cigars. .

"Oh, Muriel... Oh, my Jesus... My..."

She struggled but she was weak and only half conscious. She was held in place and before she knew or realized what had happened, it was done.

Morning came.

She woke in her own bed.

In the first few moments after opening her eyes, she wasn't sure what had happened. She only knew something *had* happened – something terrible. Then parts of the memory slowly begun to surface and she realized she had inherited a lifelong nightmare. They never said a word to each other about that night. But he began to change again, and so did she. The look was gone from his eyes and he never laid a hand on her again. He became quiet, and turned his face from her often, and he spoke very little to her for the rest of the time she was at home.

She, too, looked away.

She had begun to harbor something in her mind. It was something ugly and alive that would grow into a twisted, paralyzing shame over the years. Some confused, horrible guilt that she would never really quite understand. A cancer that had taken root in her soul and was growing into fears, suspicions, irrational thoughts, and…nightmares.

"Dad," she said now, "it's me, Muriel."

He didn't move.

"Dad, I saw Mom today, finally."

He remained still.

"I can't stay, but I have to tell you something. I know what's happened to you. I…I know that all those years ago you destroyed both of our lives."

His blue eyes seemed to sparkle in the sunlight.

"I...got pregnant that night, Dad. But I never had the baby. I couldn't. I had an abortion and I thought that would fix things. I thought it would make me clean again, but it made me worse. And since then nothing has worked.

I couldn't face Mom. I'm sorry. I couldn't come home or she would have known, I'm sure. I...I met a wonderful man. I'm getting married. I'm going to tell him now. Everything. I hope he'll understand. I think he will. He loves me a lot...and Dad...I know you didn't mean it and...I forgive you."

He never moved a muscle.

And that was okay with Muriel.

THIRTY-TWO

Immediately after hanging up from the call informing him of Muriel's whereabouts, Balk picked up the phone and dialed. The familiar female voice answered. "Well, hello," Balk said.

"Hello. More troubles?"

"Just one more issue, I think."

"Out west?"

"Yes."

"And?"

"I remember a...vision you once shared, a very colorful, crazy kind of...60's dream. Do you recall that?"

"Yes."

"Well, I think it's appropriate that we share that vision again."

"I understand."

"But we have to go immediately. The information I'm getting tells me we only have a short time."

"The city?"

"La Quinta, California."

"One moment, please."

Balk heard what sounded like papers shuffling. Then the line was put on hold. After several moments the woman returned. "Do we have a minimum of three hours?" she asked.

"Yes, I believe so. But not much more."

"I'll take the information now," the voice said.

———————

Two hours later, a telephone company work van pulled up to the curb in front of Muriel's apartment. Two men got out of the vehicle, opened the van's sliding, side door and put on tool belts, complete with telephone test sets, meters and other technical looking test gear. Both were young, clean cut and wearing official telephone company I.D. badges.

After opening a telephone cross-connection terminal box near the curb, one man attached his test set to the connections as if making a call or testing a line. The other returned to the truck and began jotting notes on what appeared to be a work order.

A elderly woman approached them. "My phone has been acting up for months," she said. "I get all this static, especially at night."

"That's why we're here, ma'am. We think it's a corroded cable line. We've had several reports so we're going to see if we can get this cleaned up for you."

"It's about time." the woman said, and turned back toward her door.

Moments later, the man doing paperwork left the truck and walked toward the fence that bordered Muriel's small yard, patio and sliding glass door. After looking over the fence, he turned to his partner and gestured with a smile, as if he'd found the trouble spot. He stepped up to the front door and rang the bell. There was no answer. He returned to his partner, who appeared to finish his work at the terminal. The men placed a ladder against the fence at Muriel's yard. In broad daylight, one climbed over.

Entering the sliding glass door was quick and easy. The other man stood watch outside while his partner slipped inside. Five minutes later, after receiving an all clear head nod, the man inside slipped quickly out through the front door. The pair then moved the ladder away from the fence and placed their tools in the truck.

As one began doing paperwork again, the other stepped up to the front door of the woman who had approached them. He rang the bell. When she came to the door, he said, "We think we found the trouble, ma'am, and we've got it fixed temporarily. But it will take some cable work to finish the job. You'll see us back out soon, to wrap things up. Your phone okay now?"

The woman stepped to her phone and picked it up. "Actually it does sound better," she said.

"Great. Thank you ma'am."

"Thank you!" the woman said, thinking to herself what nice young men the phone company was hiring these days.

THIRTY-THREE

Jack took a long walk that evening after dinner.

The drifts of sand were turning a pale red-orange under the light from the setting sun, and long shadows stretched over the small knolls, breaking up bushy clusters of sage and scrub. Several rows of Tamarisk trees lined the distant hills beneath the mountains. It was cooling down and a slight breeze picked up. The smells of wild flowers and sage were intense, and a deep sense of calm pervaded.

Jack could hear only the slight rush of a warm breeze and the sound of his boots crunching the fine desert sand. As he walked, the questions came again like rows of ugly little ducklings in a midway shooting gallery that would not be knocked down. Weincamp? Moonmare? And now, the question of the day — Martin Balk — what part had he played in this whole affair? And, of course, there was still Muriel. How was she? What had he really done to her? Was she hurting?

After a solitary fifty minutes of intense mental inventory Jack decided what he had to do. And he felt he knew who he could trust to help him. He returned to his room, picked up the phone, and dialed Pike. It was 8:10 P.M.

"Hello, Pike here."

"John, this is Jack Moore."

"Hi, Jack. Somehow I thought I might hear from you."

"Really? How come?"

"I don't know. You just seemed, well, a little uneasy, I guess, again today."

"Actually, John, the more I find out about this whole business, the more uneasy I get."

"Anything I can do for you?"

"Yeah. I think so. Can I come over and talk?"

"Sure thing."

———————

He and Pike shared a scotch.

Jack took a swallow, not a sip. The whiskey bit at the back of his throat. He held back a cough and took a deep breath. Then he placed the glass down on Pike's coffee table and calmly said, "I want out, John."

Pike was shocked. "Out *completely*?... Like send me home, out?"

"That's right."

"But why, Jack? I know there's some danger involved with this and it's not your everyday outing but, Christ, I thought this is what guys like you waited lifetimes for."

"We do. And that's exactly what I've been struggling with since I've been here. But something's not right, John."

"What do mean, not right?"

"I mean *really* not right. Like illegal not right, and inhumane. And frankly, you're about the only guy here I really feel comfortable telling this to."

"Well, I appreciate your confidence, believe me. But what do you mean, illegal?"

"John, I don't care what anybody says, I get the strong feeling there's more to Andrew Weincamp's death than a guy who's a little off center committing murder then suicide."

"I told you what a kook he was, Jack, and remember, he had just found out Moonmare had a fatal flaw. His baby was suddenly in big trouble."

"Right, but it seems like that would give a man like him just one more challenge to dig into. I mean, you spend a lifetime creating this incredible living organism and because it's overweight you kill yourself? I doubt it."

"So what do think?"

"There's some sort of cover up. That's what I think. And here's the punch line. Strange as it may sound, I think Balk is involved."

Pike burst out with a stunned laugh. "The *Vice President?*"

"I know it sounds crazy, John, but hear me out. He was closest to Weincamp during the whole Moonmare development, from what I can figure out. And you know I've been thinking, if he was more than just a little involved, maybe even *responsible* for the project, he'd stand to lose a lot these days if a kook like Weincamp got a little fed up and started flapping his jaw, right?"

"Jack, do you realize you're implicating the Vice President of the United States in a murder cover up?"

"But it fits!" Jack said. "And then this nuclear business. It seems like overkill to me. I mean, if Moonmare is what we're all saying — just a God-damned meat machine — then why all the fuss? Sure, they may want to get rid of her, but a nuclear explosion on the moon, for Christ-sakes? What the hell makes everybody — and *particularly* the man running for President right now — so anxious to vaporize the thing?"

Pike pondered this question. Jack sensed that he may have been swayed slightly. "You got anything more than just speculation on this, Jack?" he asked.

"No, I don't, but I've got a life to lead and it doesn't include being an accomplice to something like this. I've got other priorities these days."

Pike put his scotch down and got up. He paced for a few seconds, then turned back to Jack. "Jack, I think you're over reacting, buddy," he said. "I think you've just been handed a whole lot to swallow and you're having a hard time getting it all down."

"I want out, John. I mean it. Can you arrange it or do I need to go higher?"

Pike poured Jack another scotch. "Here," he said, "have another snort and relax. Let me send up for a Valium to get you a good night's sleep. Just give it tonight. Then let's have breakfast and talk in the morning."

"It's not sleep I need, John, it's out of here. I'm sorry."

"Jack, do you realize what this is going to do to the mission? We'll have to bring in someone new and maybe start all over!"

"I've been here less than a week, now. You can get a replacement and you know it."

"Listen—"

"John, I want out."

Pike saw there was no changing his mind. He finished his scotch and placed the glass on the bar. "Wait here," he said, "I need to make a call." He walked into an adjacent room.

The moment Pike left Jack began to feel panicky. Had he really done the right thing? What would this do to his military status? Probably destroy it, he decided, but that was okay. What mattered at this point was just getting home to Muriel and starting their new life. Muriel. And Cal. He had hurt them terribly. It seemed like months since he had heard her voice or stroked Cal's reddish coat.

He got to his feet, poured another scotch, and drank most of it in one gulp. He began to pace. He felt slightly light-headed and put the glass back on the bar. As he moved around the room he stepped into Pike's office cubicle. On the desk the computer was up on the ASNA intranet browser.

On impulse, he sat down and began to type…

In a room close by, John Pike had just finished dialing a familiar telephone number. A male voice answered. "Hello."

"Hi," Pike said.

"Hi, John. Problem?"

"Yes, sir. A big problem."

"Lieutenant Colonel Moore, again?"

"Yes."

"We've begun to suspect that. Hang on. I want to put us into record here, then I'd like you to run it down for me." There were several clicks, then a series of beeps began. The voice returned. "Okay, John, tell us all about it. And go through it in detail." Pike began. He relayed everything Jack had said and done.

———

Twenty minutes later Pike came back into the room and found Jack standing at the bar, scotch in hand.

As soon as Pike entered Jack sensed something had changed. The look on Pike's face was not warm and friendly any more. It was business. "Have a seat, Jack," he said flatly.

Jack sat down.

"I've just had a conversation with the...'head office', you might say."

"And?"

"And they think you should reconsider. They feel you've come too far at this point to back out."

"John, I told you. I've been reconsidering since the minute I set foot in this place. There's nothing more to think about."

"There's quite a bit more to think about, Jack."

Jack suddenly sensed another subtle shift in Pike's demeanor. The statement he had just made wasn't simply business, it contained the hint of a threat. Jack stared at him. "Like what?" he finally said.

"Well, for starters, your military career. You realize this would go on your record."

"I'm going to be retiring, John. I just hadn't told anyone."

"But you want out with honor, don't you, Jack?"

"A *dishonorable?*"

"Jack, the security of the country is involved here. This is not small potatoes. And you made a commitment."

"But my record is excellent and you know it. That's one reason I'm here."

"Right."

"And you also know a dishonorable discharge would ruin any future of mine in commercial air work."

"Yes."

Jack slammed down the glass. He was furious. "Okay. If that's the way they want to play it, fine. I'll fight it. I'll bank on the courts to see it my way."

"But that's no good either, Jack, because the courts can't find out about this."

"So what the hell is this? Now I have no rights?"

"Jack, you knew this was top secret when you took the job. You're no newcomer. You're well aware of what the word classified means. Now all you have to do is finish what you've started."

"Classified, right. That I knew. But nobody said it meant going to the moon with a nuclear bomb. And I don't recall the stipulation about assisting in a murder cover up!"

"That's pure speculation, Jack. And frankly, it's not particularly wise to keep repeating."

Jack was right. He had been right all along and with this last statement of Pike's he now knew it. But there was more. Pike had been a fake, too. He was one of them. As friendly and sincere as this man had seemed, all along it had been a facade.

Jack swore to himself. How could he have been so gullible and not seen it? "You know, John," he said, "I've been doubting myself all along with these suspicions. I've been feeling guilty and unsure and thinking I was just paranoid. But I'm believing in myself more and more with every word that comes out of your mouth."

"Jack, listen. Will you just calm down and—"

"Bullshit! I'm out of here." He started for the door. "Jack, you realize your military record was just one of several factors involved in your recruitment for this mission."

Jack stopped in his tracks.

"We also selected you based on some aspects of your personal life."

"Meaning?" Jack said, turning to face Pike.

"Meaning that when we brought you in on this we thought you were basically…unattached. Free to make

your own choices. Unhampered by…personal relation-
ships."

Jack stared into Pike's eyes. Suddenly he realized
that this man's lack of sincerity was just scratching the
surface. These were the eyes of a killer. Muriel was in
grave danger.

"How did you know about her?"

"Evidently she called in for you in the middle of
the night. She sounded a little upset. That prompted
some… background research."

"Is she okay?" he asked in a quavering voice.

Pike smiled. The kindness and sincerity were back.
"At the moment, I believe she's fine."

THIRTY-FOUR

On the way back to his room, Jack passed by the door to the linen room. It was ajar as it had been before and no one was in sight. He could see the payphone within twenty feet.

Again, acting on impulse, he walked in, picked up the receiver, dropped in a few coins and dialed Muriel. After what seemed like an eternity a mechanical voice said, "Please deposit seventy-five cents." He fumbled quickly in his pocket and came up with another handful of change. Plenty of quarters. He shoved two in but the third dropped on the floor. It clanked and went rolling away into a pile of white towels.

He looked around on the verge of panic. Still no one.

He shoved in another quarter.

The voice said, "Thank you."

"Finally," Jack whispered, "God, finally!" After another long wait there was a ring.

When the phone rang Muriel was in the bathroom, just finishing removing her makeup. She had been home for just over an hour. Though she was completely beat, she felt like a new woman.

The trip had been the most difficult one of her life, but it had been worth it. She felt clean, relieved, and totally renewed. An incredible load had been lifted from her soul. She was also totally confident that Jack loved and would return to her, and she was now prepared to simply bide her time and wait patiently for that day.

Since her hands and face were greasy with cream, on the first ring she considered letting her machine pick it up and calling back later. Then she decided she could probably get her hands clean and make it to the bedside phone in time to take the call.

She quickly rinsed them.

It rang a second time.

She reached for a towel and began drying.

It rang again. On the next ring the machine would pick it up. She ran, still drying her hands, toward the bedside table.

When she picked up the receiver and placed it to her ear something strange happened.

Her answering machine was clicking on at the same instant. She heard the beginning of her usual message, "Hello this is 555 —" but then there was a scraping noise of some sort, and what sounded like the very end of a male voice saying, "—ack." Immediately following this she heard what sounded like other voices in the background, then another click. Then the line reverted to dial tone.

She hung up, considered what she had just heard, and played back her machine. It hadn't been Jack's voice, she was sure. But was it someone else's voice or just noises on the line?

Was someone saying the end of Jack's name? And whose were the other voices? Or could it have been just a weird connection, a click, or something on the line that just sounded like the end of the word Jack?

Suddenly she thought of the general the other night, asking for her name and location. Again she envisioned the grim, pockmarked face. She got to her feet. "No," she said out loud to herself. "Don't do this, Muriel!"

She marched back to the bathroom saying out loud, "Do not start again! He's fine! He's a big boy and he can take care of himself. And he loves you and damn it, stop this! He'll be back! He'll be back!"

And by the time she reached the bathroom mirror she saw terror rising up in her eyes. "Oh, God," she said, "please Jack, not again!"

During those same few moments Jack stood in the linen room beside John Pike. Pike had just finished taking the phone receiver from him and saying, "Jack, Jack, Jack…" as he hung up the phone.

Three other men had also appeared suddenly, out of nowhere. Pike had placed his hand on Jack's shoulder. He was smiling, saying, "She'll be fine, Jack. I promise. But only — now hear me, buddy — *only* if this is absolutely the last time we have these problems with you. Come on, I've got something that'll help you sleep."

THIRTY-FIVE

The phone call that evening led to a series of events of which Muriel would later have only vague memories.

The first few hours would remain very vivid — the pacing, the rationalizing, the talking out loud to herself, the attempts to sleep, the slow, inevitable build up to hysteria.

She would also remember taking a sleeping pill later. One of the strong ones Cynthia had told her to keep handy for these types of situations. But it would only be much later that she would remember thinking to herself that the pills in the bottle looked different somehow, smaller than she had previously remembered them.

It was shortly after taking the pill when things began to blur. At first there was sleep, yes, but a strange very awkward kind of sleep. A sleep that was full of brilliant, bizarre colors and straining and pulling — not in her body, but in her mind. A kind of 1930's horror, comic book sleep that swept over her with a frightening sense of reality.

That led to the dream, the worst one yet — the most frightening and realistic nightmare she would later remember, of her entire life. The hands were huge and inside her like bony clumps of rotten flesh. They pushed up high into her stomach and it felt like they were drenched in acid, trying to sear away her lungs and heart.

Sour beer dripped into her face.

"Oh, God, Mur, hon...the heat...."

A face was there, too. A doctor's face, above her in the light. It was twisted and withered with cracked, bleeding skin. It glared directly at Muriel and the look in its eyes was of hysteria and murder.

And in this dream there was a baby — her baby. Her aborted fetus. It had been cut into pieces. Its extremities lay glowing in a wash of bright fluorescent colors — each tiny arm and leg still moving. The toes curling. The fingers no bigger than peanuts, clasping, reaching. The doctor stood above the tiny bleeding limbs, colors streaming from his skin. He began to shudder and weep as he worked with a bloody scalpel... At some time later there were horrible screams, shattering glass, streets and red flashing ambulance lights.

Then, as the dream began to open into reality, Cynthia's face was close to hers, whispering something about "...poor thing." The psychiatrist's head was swollen and deformed, glowing like an animated freak, pumpkin monster. It was swimming in a sea of brilliant waving, vibrating musical notes. Somewhere in the glare and blinding wash of colors, an injection followed and sirens and sterile gowns and for a while it seemed like the dream was coming back, over and over in waves of bright unthinkable horror. There were lights like the sun and moon and faces drifting through the glare.

"...So fucking hot...Mur, honey...oh, yeah... Jesus, yeah."

And more straining, this time in both her body and her mind. There were shrieks and cigar smoke and tremendous birds and throngs of frogs chirruping in the hot, sticky, humid night.

Finally, much later, after what seemed like a long, long time, darkness seeped in — the beginning of real sleep. The hands with their heat and pressure and lumpiness were gone, and she had somehow filled with cool, gentle shadows — a long, peaceful stream of nothingness that was just like she had once imagined it might be like in the depths of space.

THIRTY-SIX

For Jack and the others the next several weeks were a rigorous grind of field training, conditioning, and classroom sessions. Driven by the knowledge that Muriel's life was in danger if he did not comply with every aspect of the mission, Jack made no further attempts to talk to Pike or to be released. He also said nothing to Tiller, Polling or Ericson. At first he considered telling them secretly and trying to form an alliance. But he wasn't sure Tiller's red neck views would allow him to believe or sympathize with Jack's story, and Polling was so young there was no telling which way she would go. He almost confided in Ericson, but in the end decided it was just too risky.

The one thing he did do was obtain Pike's word that if he complied entirely and kept total secrecy for the remainder of his lifetime, Muriel would remain unharmed and he would be allowed to retire honorably, immediately following the mission. He and Muriel would be left alone to start their new life. With this knowledge and the hope for the future that it created, Jack simply focused on the task at hand and put his nose to the grindstone. He trained hard, said little, and bore inside the guilt he felt for having left behind the woman who loved and depended on him.

THIRTY-SEVEN

The schedule called for the next week to be dedicated to training in explosives handling and deployment. Jack learned there were a total of nine explosive charges, each the size of a small suitcase. They would be carried to the moon in a sealed, unarmed state. Tiller and Jack would simply place them on the ground in the Corral in a pattern that virtually assured at least one of the charges would be in kill range for the Mare as she moved through the area toward the Caller.

Once armed, any charge could be set off in two ways. One was simply by touch. If the Mare stepped on one or bumped it with a hoof, a motion sensitive trigger would ignite it instantly. The other means of ignition was by an electronic signal that would be sent from the Barn control room by Tiller.

The sending unit was also a suitcase-sized box. It was an extremely simple package to use. With its lid opened it contained two rows of nine buttons — an upper row of "ARM" switches and a lower row of "IGNITE" switches.

The unit would be carried to the control room by Tiller on the day of confrontation. Tiller would depress each of the "ARM" buttons just prior to the Mare's entrance into the Chute. This would arm all the units and allow him to quickly hit the proper "IGNITE" switches as she came forward.

Part of the week also involved geographic familiarization. This consisted mostly of a series of field exercises carried out entirely at night. The men worked at a mock desert North Forty area built to scale to the actual lunar area. Under the stars they covered and recovered every inch of the same steps they would soon take on the moon.

Following this came a period of intense cramming on the technical aspects of the mission — equipment operation, familiarization, and checkout. During this time the group engaged in repetitive exercises and run downs of each of the seventeen test sequences they would go through as the mission progressed.

The final segment was dedicated to safety and alternative action plans. The men were placed in emergency situations and expected to utilize the proper safety equipment, standardized procedures and sound judgment to successfully overcome nearly any hazard they might encounter. This included the possibility of everything from a leaky life support suit and failure of several of the explosive charges to possible unexpected reactions from the Mare in the moments following umbilical shutdown.

When the training had been completed, Jack felt ready. Though the guilt and fear for Muriel persisted, a sense of excitement and anticipation had also filled his thoughts. The games were over. The simulations had been run until he could perform them blindfolded in his sleep. As his father had said some thirty-five years ago, his turn had come.

THIRTY-EIGHT

When the main engines first fired on the Ganymede VII booster rocket, the roar of 1.5 million pounds of thrust leaped out of the earth like a volcano. Then, exactly two seconds after it began, the four engines went from one quarter to full throttle. The Ganymede groaned and shook and lifted off its pad with a tremendous shudder.

The rocket gained altitude and speed quickly. Pinned to his seat, Jack felt as if he were being hurled on some tremendous, cosmic catapult. The initial thrust continued for another two minutes and forty seconds. The shaking was sometimes violent, but Jack, Tiller and Polling were too busy with systems monitoring and mid-launch checks to pay much attention. Six minutes later, at separation of the rocket's second stage, they were approaching earth orbit. It was during this time that even with the force pushing upward from beneath him, Jack began to feel a change in his body's density. They were approaching the fringes of the earth's immediate gravitational umbrella, and each of the cells in his body knew it.

When the Pinto escape module separated from the Ganymede VII's third stage, there was a tremendous shock. For a moment Jack was afraid the rocket might actually be coming apart from the force of the blast. But a second later only a slight rumble remained and the third stage hull of the huge two hundred and eighty foot monster that had slung them upward began falling back toward the earth, burning up as it went.

Complete thrust shutdown took place eleven minutes and thirty-three seconds after lift-off. It was then that Jack experienced, for the first time, the full sensation of complete gravitational absence.

The feeling was incredible.

Suddenly the upward force died away, but there was no familiar pull back to earth. They had reached a shelf of nothingness and all sense of speed and power seemed to have slipped behind them, falling back to earth with the Ganymede booster.

He had arrived.

He was in space and on his way to the moon.

Minutes later he, Tiller and Polling had gotten to work. They began with a precise firing sequence of the tiny, computer controlled CAR's — Capsule Adjustment Rockets. After two more hours they had positioned Pinto into the three revolution slingshot orbit it would need to gain the escape velocity and the trajectory necessary for their lunar journey.

Following these corrections, Jack floated away from the two men to the Section Two control panel and pushed a series of buttons. The three porthole shields that had covered the Pinto's windows slid back. Beneath the men the earth hung like a huge, slow-moving marble, coated with brilliant blues, browns, and whites. The southern tip of South America curled like a giant parrot's beak rotating toward the horizon. Cloud patterns streaked the globe in swirls and arcs of wispy white tendrils. A hazy, glowing, life-giving layer of atmosphere held tightly to the surface. The entire immense ball was both turning on its axis and, as the craft moved toward one of the farthest arc points in its orbit, it was also slowly growing smaller.

For thirty-two hours they orbited — gained speed and position for the two hundred and forty thousand mile ride ahead.

Then they fired the escape sequence.

Pinto was slung free into deep space.

During the following hours Jack watched the brilliant blue and white ball that had dominated his view grow smaller and smaller as the blackness of space before them was replaced with the glowing, white, ruptured face of the moon.

THIRTY-NINE

Twenty-one days after his attempted phone call to Muriel, Jack Moore stood on the moon, quietly peering out through the heat shielded window of Bunkhouse.

Though he was not conscious of them, there were two types of sounds very close by. One was Tiller's voice as he talked via radio to Mission Control. The other sound was the subdued but distinctive electronic chirruping that was the digitized voice of Moonmare.

The other structures and geographical features that made up the North Forty were visible to Jack. To his immediate left was a small modular power station with rows of rectangular solar panels terraced out from its base. The station looked like a cluster of large white pipes, solar panels and pumps topped with several radar dish receivers, transmitters, and snake-like runs of electrical conduits.

Farther to his left on a distant, rocky plateau stood Caller 11. The small square near its base was pulsating a brilliant sky blue light. Directly in front of Jack was the Porch, the deck-like shelf of white metal grid work that was the stepping out ramp from the airlock of the building he and Tiller were presently in. Three metal stairs led from the Porch down to a boot worn pathway in the lunar dust nicknamed Happy Trail. Happy Trail was ninety yards long. It wound its way down a slight embankment to Jack's right and into the base of a three story tall pyramid shaped structure made almost entirely of white metal beams — the Barn. Happy Trail ended at the center of the Barn's base in front of a square elevator shaft. The shaft housed a small, open, rectangular capsule that ran from the moon's surface up to a triangular control room at the structure's top center. Directly in front of the Barn was the Corral, a four-acre circular depression framed by a natural rim of rock structures. Still farther to Jack's right, and leading away into darkness, was the Chute. It ran from the mouth of the Corral up a gentle two hundred foot long grade to the crater rim beyond.

The crater, Malkus Arrens, was seventeen kilometers in diameter. It culminated in a string of smaller craters and gullies that together made up a one hundred and ninety-six mile shallow canyon named Big Valley. On any true-to-scale moon globe the North Forty was located on the side facing away from earth, in a flat, high, finger-like section at the northwest corner of Mare Moscoviense.

Jack had now resided in Bunkhouse for three days. He had looked out of this same window on several occasions during that time and, just as at this moment, he had continually had trouble conceiving the reality of the past month.

Tiller's voice brought him out of the trance. "Hey, Jackie, get up here, buddy. We got her on visual!"

Jack turned and moved quickly up a small ramp to a circular arrangement of computer and radar screens and other communications gear. Tiller was seated at the center of a complex array of digital equipment. "Look here," he said, as he saw Jack approaching.

A greenish blip flashed on a radar screen showing the signal received by a dish mounted on a mountain top just behind and to the west of Bunkhouse. The dish had been locked in place pointing straight down Big Valley.

For the past two days this same screen had been devoid of anything alive or meaningful. Only its sweeping green line and quiet but incessant blip had reminded the men that it was on and functioning. But now it showed something amazing — a tiny, slowly advancing green dot. Something alive and conscious in the vacuum. Something coming directly toward Jack and Tiller at a slow but relentless pace.

Just before calling Jack, Tiller had been conversing with Bill Ericson. Ericson was seated in Mission Control at a console very similar to the one in Bunkhouse. His setup, however, was located on the third floor of the Saltridge Mission Command Center.

"Well," Tiller continued, "it's official, buddy, our pony is headed for the Chute."

After the few moments of static it took Ericson's voice to cross the two hundred and forty thousand mile void, the engineer's words came clearly through the speaker. "From what your tickers are doing to my vital signs readings down here, I should have known."

Tiller smiled. "Doesn't seem to be shakin' up ol' Jackie boy, here. 'Course, it takes more 'n a horse the size 'o Billy Bob's to get him uptight."

Ericson spoke again. "Got your lasso out yet, Jack?"

Tiller chuckled. "You get it on her, Jackie, and I'll hop on for a little ride."

Tiller and Ericson laughed briefly. "Al, I mark at zero six zero three hours," Ericson said, getting down to business.

Tiller checked his watch and a reading on the panel in front of him. "On the nose," he said.

"Sounds to me like she's on schedule."

Jack sat down, and with a few key strokes called up a numbered sequence on the closest computer terminal. He quickly ran a program that interfaced with the radar system. It calculated Moonmare's rate of speed and the distance she had to travel. "By my figures," he said, "she's due into the Chute in about six hours and ten minutes, give or take a few seconds."

Tiller picked up the thought. "That puts her in just after twelve hundred."

"Okay," Ericson said, "then what do you say we get busy with the list?"

"You got it," Tiller said. "Want me to lead or follow?"

"This time you lead."

"On your mark, get set, and...how about we get this going with a geo-disturbance reading of point zero, zero two."

"Sounds steady enough. Check."

"And we have an external lunar temperature reading of minus one seven zero degrees centigrade."

"Check," Ericson said again.

"Caller 11 signal frequency strength, point one niner and holding steady."

"Check."

As Tiller and Ericson continued through this final, mandatory checklist, Jack moved back to the window. He again stared out along the Chute toward the crater's rim.

Twenty minutes later everything had checked out perfectly, except for a momentary glitch in the vibration cycle generated by Caller 11. Both Tiller and Ericson agreed that this was nothing to be alarmed about. Although it was not a frequent occurrence, it had happened before. On past occasions it had been explained as due to a phenomenon known as solar molecular hierarching, a momentary reorganizing of molecules in the solar strips that gathered the Caller's operating power.

Finally, Jack heard Ericson's voice say, "I mark at zero six two three, Al. I'd call that a 'go' for all systems."

Tiller responded. "So I guess that means I gotta go pry Jackie boy away from that window and get our butts in gear."

"How about if you two guys get suited up and I'll switch to Pinto for a 'traffic update' from the sky?"

"Talk to you soon. Bunkhouse out."

"Mission Control out."

The radio went quiet.

Jack watched Tiller's reflection in the window. The lanky Texan stood up from the console. He stretched his long thin arms, then studied Jack from behind. Jack suddenly became very conscious of the chirruping of Moonmare's voice drifting quietly into the room from the ceiling speakers.

"Ready for a stroll?" Tiller finally said.

The fear slid up Jack's gut toward his throat. He turned away from the window toward Tiller. "Happy trails to you," he said.

Ahead of her, things were different. She was drawing close to something. An answer? A release? An escape? The fear had grown even more intense during the past days but so, too, had the hope. And now, in the lunar night, there was something strange — a glow ahead, a slight blush of light at a distance and above her. There was something about the light — a finality, a sense that the answer truly was at hand this time, a hope that there would not be another change, another stop leading to elation followed by the dreaded sinking back into horror and exhaustion.

Even with no mental framework or intellect to explore her feelings, Moonmare was sensing an end, at last, to a very long journey. The parts of her great dark expanse were gaining definition.

And there was something else – a heightening of the need for another being. Though she had no words or way to express what she felt, she thought that she was now heading for the place she had been destined to go all along. She was somehow sure that at that place an answer — the answer — was waiting and she should not face it alone. When the time came for her exhaustion and fear to end there should be something else, some other being close to her.

She moved forward.

She climbed the gentle slope of silver sand under clouds of stars and, through the blinding pain of her exhaustion, she felt a kind of excitement — a childish anticipation...a coming home.

FORTY

Pinto hung in orbit above the moon, manned by Polling. As the command module for this mission it did more than just carry the men to and from the earth. It had also released, and would later recapture, the landing craft, White Foal, which Tiller and Jack had taken down to the surface three days earlier. White Foal was now sitting directly over the two men on a twelve foot thick concrete pad that was also the roof of Bunkhouse.

Pinto's other purpose was to allow Polling to pass directly over the North Forty in a low lunar orbit when Moonmare arrived at the Corral. With the help of an assortment of precision video cameras, infra-red tracking gear and back-up flare rockets, she would document the entire event.

She had been listening to the conversation going on between Tiller, Moore and Ericson as she floated weightless inside Pinto making minor adjustments on the computer software panel that ran much of Pinto's camera equipment.

After hearing that the checklist had been successfully completed, she knew she would be next on the air. She had pushed herself lightly away from the control panel toward a section opening in the metal gridwork that provided the separation between Pinto's two floors. Floating through the opening she approached, and finally strapped herself into, a console that was the brain of the Pinto space craft. As she had anticipated, Ericson's voice came over one of the speakers, "You up there, Janice?"

"You bet your boots," Polling quipped, "and headed for the North Forty."

"Everything okay with our little 'eye in the sky'?"

"Couldn't be better, Bill."

"Sounds like you're ready to run your numbers and shoot a few test frames."

This was exactly what Polling had wanted to hear. "Yes, sir," she responded. "On your command."

The two then went through a basic checklist similar to the one covered previously between Ericson and Tiller. All systems were functioning perfectly.

As the list was completed, Pinto was approaching an area in space above the moon's terminator — the separation line between day and night. The craft had been passing over the day side and was now moving toward the dark.

In order to shoot the test frames, Ericson decided that Polling would send a cluster of laser guided, Ladybug flare rockets down to a location just across the dark side of the terminator. As the flares ignited, Polling would snap a series of photos and record video footage. To test these imaging functions, and Polling's ability to lock in on specific areas quickly, she and Ericson worked in a series of segmented grid arrangements.

On monitors in front of them, both could see the surface of the moon from Pinto's position in the sky. Now, as they were about to begin, each activated a computer program that superimposed a series of luminous grid lines over their screens. These were generated by the Ladybug guidance system.

Ericson began. "Okay, Janice, how about on the terminator, peak quadrant, grids zero, niner apple, by seven, one, zebra."

Polling immediately began to key the numbers into her system. "How many?" she asked.

"How about a cluster of four. 'Walk' 'em about two miles into the dark."

"Coming right up," Polling said.

Using a series of activation commands, she opened a panel on the side of Pinto and extended a jointed mechanical arm carrying a cluster of twenty-seven Ladybug rockets. The arm swiveled into a firing position calculated by the guidance system grid layout.

The tubes rotated.

In a matter of seconds the whole arrangement had locked into place.

Polling selected the number of rockets and designated which of the twenty-seven tubes would fire. "Ladybugs off," she said, and pushed the "Fire" button.

Four small rockets left the tubes in a staggered burst. "How long?" Ericson asked.

"Should be about…a hundred and ninety seconds."

"Good. In the meantime, give me a few shots of the day side. Grid zero, seven charley, by six, one, zebra."

Again Polling went to work on the keyboard. This time a different arm extended from Pinto with four cameras mounted on it. Two were live action video cameras. The other two took digital still images. One video and one still camera were fitted with high resolution, telephoto lenses.

As Polling finished entering the numbers the cameras locked in. "Focal lengths?" she asked.

"Whatever you like," Ericson responded. "I have a small peak above that ridge - upper right quadrant – apple, apple. Can you bring it in?"

"That one?" Polling said as she zoomed the camera's lens in for a closer angle. The image drew forward on Ericson's monitor, bringing the area into precise focus.

"Damn, you do nice work!" the engineer spouted.

"Only the best for you, Bill."

"In that case, give us a capture on that and go southeast. Center quadrant. I've got a row of what looks like three small craters at seven Charlie."

Polling's fingers flew. The cameras captured digital images. The information was immediately transmitted to Saltridge on earth. The jointed arm then swiveled and moved the cameras to the new location. "There's number one," she said, "and numbers two and three coming southeast," as she instructed the arm to pan the cameras across the three craters Ericson had selected.

"Excellent, Janice. You are truly an artist, my friend."

"Don't mention it."

"Capture and send those. How about our Lady-bugs?"

"Approaching impact," Polling said. "Coming around for the light show."

Her fingers keyed numbers. The arm swiveled. Cameras locked, zoomed, and focused.

The images Ericson saw on earth were spectacular. In the middle of an area of darkness just across the ter-minator, the Ladybug rockets began to ignite, creating tiny, silent circles of white light. The instant the first cir-cle appeared, one camera zoomed in revealing a group of jagged peaks bordered by a small canyon and two cra-ters. The entire image was bathed in white light that was now beginning to slowly fade to an orange color.

The second rocket ignited close to the first, slight-ly overlapping its ring of light. This revealed another group of craters and the end of the canyon running up from the lower circle. The third ignited, as did the fourth, in overlapping circles of first white, then orange, and eventually deep red light. When the fourth shot was at its peak, the first was fading to a dark purple and fi-nally back to darkness.

"Beautiful! Looks like you're ready to go, Cowgirl," Ericson said.

Polling smiled with pride, saying "Let's get 'er done!"

FORTY-ONE

When the seal broke and the airlock door slid open, what lay before Jack was a black, grey, and silver world with a silent beauty that defied description. Though he and Tiller had been out before setting charges in the Corral, the experience now was as exciting as if it were his first.

As he stepped out of the Bunkhouse airlock onto the white grillwork terrace of the Porch, above him were clusters of stars nearly as thick as cumulous storm clouds on earth. He immediately began to find constellations: Andromeda, her thigh buried in a swath of sparking light; Cassiopeia, seated on a star cloud; the Big Dipper, its panhandle stuck into a mountain of tiny glittering points, Sagittarius, its bow pulled taut, pointing out from one of the great spiraled arms of the Milky Way.

When Tiller's hand touched his shoulder it broke Jack's trance. The Texan's voice, partially garbled by radio transmission, conveyed a ring of excitement that told Jack he was experiencing the same incredible feeling. "Not a bad view, huh, Jackie boy?"

"Not bad at all."

"Kinda makes all the schools and pools and centrifuges and all the rest of that stuff worthwhile, don't it?"

"It sure does."

Then, as Jack glanced toward the crater rim, he became aware of a deep, rhythmic vibration in the framework he was standing on. His first thought was of the Caller. He turned to his left, and sure enough it was there on the plateau. A bright blue square of light pulsated at its base. But Jack noticed the cyclic rhythm of the blue light was out of sync with the vibration he was feeling. After a moment he realized it was not the Caller he was sensing at all. He was feeling vibrations from the hooves of Moonmare! He matched the cycle of the vibrations to how he imagined her in a full gallop. He could see her in his mind's eye — a huge stocky zebra — galloping in long, slow motion strides through the lunar night.

Again, Tiller broke the trance. "Let's get a move on," he said, "before we use up all our oxygen standin' here gawkin' at the sights."

Looking into the oval, gold tinted window of his face mask Jack gave Tiller the thumbs up sign.

"I'll go first," Tiller said.

Jack let him move by, then started forward out onto the

Porch himself. Both men moved with the same graceful skipping motion they had been taught back home in the bottoms of ASNA pools. It was the most stable and comfortable means of navigating in a gravity environment one sixth that of the earth's. Jack took two gentle, sweeping skip-steps and moved up behind Tiller. Both men skipped once more and arrived at the short stairway leading down to the moon's surface and Happy Trail.

Ericson could see both men on his monitor. "Watch your step, Al," he said, noting the detonator suitcase in the Texan's hand.

"No problem," Tiller said. "Just give me a second, here," He maneuvered to the edge of the top step, turned around facing Jack, and took hold of one of the rails. He eased one of his huge, white boots down onto the first step. Carefully, slowly, he moved the next boot down and several moments later he placed his boot on the moon's soil and felt it crunch beneath his weight. He pulled his other foot down, stepped back from the rail, and looked up at Jack. "Piece o' cake," he said. "Take your time with it."

Jack followed the same pattern. He moved to the edge, turned around, gasped both rails, and began to place one foot at a time. The first went fine. Then came the second.

"No problem," he said to himself as he was about to place his final boot on the surface. It was then that he heard a half whispered exclamation back on earth from Ericson. "Jesus!" the engineer said.

For an instant, Jack wondered what could be wrong. Then he and Tiller felt a kind of hollow sensation rise suddenly up out of the ground — a deep inaudible rumble. In the next second, the rail began swaying and Jack held tight to keep his balance. The motion seemed to subside for a moment, then returned with an even harder ground shift, this time nearly a jolt. Jack grasped the rail harder and steadied himself. He felt Tiller's hand on his waist, steadying him, but also holding on. At the same time he heard Tiller say, "What the fu—"

Ericson's voice interrupted. "Hang on...just hang on there," he exclaimed.

Both men did exactly that for several more seconds. Another rise and fall seemed to come in the cycle, then the swaying faded away. The deep cyclic rumbling still vibrated beneath them, but the moonquake was gone.

Tiller spoke up. "What the hell we got going here, Bill?" he said.

"Slight quake," Ericson responded.. Then with a chuckle, "Nothing to get too...'shook' about."

The men shared laugh. "We got one hell of a big pony comin' our way here, buddy," Tiller said.

"What were the geo disturbance readings, Bill?" Jack asked.

"Up several points," Ericson said, "but they fell back off. I think we're okay. You guys all right?"

Both men acknowledged.

"Okay, then," Tiller said. "Let's move it." He and Jack started slowly out away from the Bunkhouse porch. Ahead of them lay an expanse of bright silver ground leading to the huge pyramid tower — the Barn.

As the men moved on, Ericson re-checked and re-calculated the geographical disturbance readings they had just experienced. He hadn't wanted to relay his concerns to Tiller and Jack, but concerned he was. His numbers still showed the Mare 24 kilometers out and coming steady. Had her approach caused the quake, he wondered? And if so, what would happen when she got in close?

He made a note of the time and disturbance reading increase in his log, double checked the men's vital signs, which were now dropping to normal for the activity they were involved in, and watched as they skipped gracefully out across the pale ground.

FORTY-TWO

As Ericson monitored both astronaut's progress, he was unaware that outside on the grounds at Saltridge a black Mercedes sedan and two black SUVs had driven up and positioned themselves near the helipad. Minutes later the lights of a helicopter appeared in the night sky. It moved in from the east and landed on the helipad beside the observatory. Martin Balk exited the helicopter and was ushered into the Mercedes. As it moved off toward the Saltridge installation the SUVs followed. The helicopter lifted off, rose back into the night sky, and moved away into the stars.

Balk was taken to a little used entrance at Saltridge and ushered up several flights of stairs. There he turned to the two men that accompanied him. "Okay guys, I'm good from here. You can wait in the Level "C" conference area."

As the men disappeared around a corner, Balk moved through a series of corridors, up another flight of stairs, and finally arrived at a "T" junction. On his right, several yards away, was the door to the linen area Jack Moore had entered two weeks ago. Balk passed it, turned left, and reached John Pike's door. It was open. When he stepped in Pike was ready. "I'm all set to head down."

"Good," Balk said. "How we doing?"

"So far, so good."

"Everything on schedule?"

"Down to the minute."

The two left Pike's room and moved along the corridor. As they did, Pike updated Balk on the progress of the mission. He told Balk of the checklist status, the quake, and finished by saying, "They're on their way to the Barn now."

"About two hours left," Balk said.

"Yup. And she's on time. Running her ass off."

After several turns the pair came to an elevator marked "Secure". Pike removed a two inch plastic tube from his pocket, roughly the diameter of a pencil. He slipped it into a small nearby wall receptacle and placed his left eye to a scanner. The "up" and "down" indicators on the elevator lit up. He pushed the down arrow. The doors opened. The men entered and started down.

"How about Moore?" Balk asked.

"Not a peep out of him."

"He got the message?"

"The magic word was 'Muriel'," Pike said with a hint of pride in his voice.

Balk chuckled and shook his head.

Pike smiled. "How's she doing, by the way? Still under heavy sedation?"

"Over the edge, I'm told."

Balk thought about this for a moment. "And you know," he finally said, "I don't even think it was the LSD we slipped her. She's so God-damned neurotic I think she would have done the job on herself in a few more days anyway."

The elevator doors opened and they stepped out. They were now in a concrete tunnel instead of a corridor. They moved straight ahead, came to a short stairway, and descended.

At the bottom was a heavy, metal, red, vault-like door. Pike reached into his pocket and again pulled out the plastic tube. He inserted it in the receptacle and again placed his eye to a scanner. A recorded audio message asked, "Name, please?"

"Cowhand," Pike said.

"Thank you," the voice said.

Balk also stepped up to the scanner. After a pause, the "voice" spoke again. "Name, please?"

Balk said, "Sharp Shooter."

"Thank you. One moment, please."

The system quickly analyzed the two passwords, matching them to the appropriate voice patterns and iris prints. The vault-like door opened and the two men entered. They stepped into a small, dark control room very similar to the one Bill Ericson was seated in two floors above them. When Pike moved to a bank of equipment and threw a single switch, monitors and several banks of equipment began lighting up. Twenty minutes later the men were seated comfortably, each with a cup of coffee, watching Jack and Tiller approach the base of the Barn on the TV monitors before them. They could also see Ericson seated at his console, and they viewed the aerial images transmitted from Pinto which was now approaching its position above the North Forty.

"Almost time," Balk said. "Finally."

Pike hit a button and a digital clock countdown readout appeared on a screen in front of him. "Ninety-two minutes and fifty seconds," he said, "assuming her speed stays constant."

A few seconds later, however, both men found that was not to be the case.

FORTY-THREE

Jack and Tiller were approaching the towering Barn when it happened. At first it was barely perceptible to Jack, a sensation he couldn't quite put his finger on that something had changed. Tiller experienced the same sensation. Both men hesitated for a moment. They were about to turn and look at each other when Ericson's voice came on, "Christ! Again?" he said.

"Everything okay, Bill?" Tiller asked.

Immediately following these words it became apparent to both astronauts what was happening. The constant rumbling under their feet had disappeared. The Mare had stopped in her tracks.

A dead, still, emptiness hung over them.

Ericson's exclamation had been the result of a reading that told him Caller 11 had suddenly gone down. It was no shift in molecules, and no phenomena. It was a problem — a big one. He immediately began entering a series of instructions into the system to attempt to activate a reset program. At the same time he said, "The Caller's down, hang on a second."

When he heard this, Jack looked over his shoulder at the plateau in the distance. He could still make out the square at the Caller's base. The blue light was gone. The square was black. Dead stillness. During the eerie moments that followed, Jack thought about Moonmare. What was happening in her mind? Was she relieved? Did she, in whatever consciousness she had, realize that for the moment she was out of danger? That no predator was at her heels? He wasn't sure why, but he thought she did sense it, and he was glad for her.

Muriel also came to Jack's mind at that moment. She, too, deserved peace, he thought. In some odd way she was like Moonmare — running through her own life, constantly afraid and threatened. She deserved to stop torturing herself and shed the insecurities that haunted her like a terrible shroud. At that moment, he longed terribly to touch her face and hold her –- to tell her it would all be okay very soon. Then, as quickly as her image had swept over him, it was gone. He regained focus, knowing he had to finish what he was about to do and get back to her as quickly as possible.

It was then that he felt motion begin again under his feet. It started with one definite shudder, then another, and it finally grew into the familiar pattern. He looked back over his shoulder. The blue light on the Caller was on.

The Mare was running again. She had reared up on her hind legs, Jack thought. She had been jolted up in fear and then had started forward.

Tiller's voice broke the silence. "She's movin'," he said. "Hear me, Bill?"

"Right," Ericson said. "We're back in business."

"What the hell happened?" Tiller asked.

"I hate to say it, gents, but Caller 11 just took a momentary dump on us."

"Is it okay?"

"I reset it. It looks fine now. Full cycle and going strong."

"What's your call?" Tiller asked.

"Probably a fluke. But I want to explore some other possibilities here. In the meantime, let's push ahead."

Jack and Tiller turned to each other. They both displayed the thumbs up sign and headed once again for the elevator in the base structure of the Barn.

As the men moved on, Ericson scribbled out a series of notes. After several minutes he made a decision. He picked up the telephone beside him and dialed two digits. After one ring, Pike's voice answered, "Yes?"

"Ericson here. We're nearing confrontation and I've got two problems. I'd like a confirmation for continuance, sir."

"What's happening, Bill?" Pike said.

"Two things, sir. First, the geo disturbance readings are several points over projection. Things are really starting to shake up there. I should have a point zero-two-one at this time. Instead I've got a point zero-five-four."

"I see. And?"

"And Caller 11 just went down. That's my main concern."

"Have you been able to discern why?"

"Not sure. Maybe the vibrations. It's been acting a bit erratic."

"And the current situation?"

"I was able to reset it, but like I said, things are going to get a hell of a lot more shaky up there pretty soon now."

"And the crew?"

"On schedule and moving in. They're about to start up to the control center in the Barn."

"And your recommendation, Bill?"

Ericson knew there were two choices. Either push ahead or go for an alternate, which would mean aborting the mission, probably temporarily. In such a case he would activate Caller 3 and have the Mare reverse her direction. While she was moving away he would re-check and verify Caller 11's integrity. Once it had been verified, he would restart the mission. If the Caller's integrity could not be confirmed, he would recommend a full mission abort. They would have to try again another day. After weighing all the ramifications in his mind, Ericson said, "I'd say go for the alternate, sir. Send her off toward Caller 3 and re-check the situation. Then bring her back in."

"Thank you, Bill," Pike said. "Please hold."

Pike pushed the hold button and looked at Balk.

"Straight ahead," Balk said.

After several minutes of idle conversation to make Ericson think a real conversation had gone on, Pike released the hold button. "Hi, Bill," he said. "Listen, we very much appreciate your quick assessment of the situation, but we're confident the reset should hold and we're electing to move ahead."

Ericson had figured this would be the case. "Sure," he said, "I just hope things hold together up there."

"We're sure they will."

"Okay."

Ericson shook his head as he hung up. "Sure thing, sir," he whispered to himself.

———————

Tiller and Jack entered the elevator and started up. It was a thirty-five foot climb in an open metal cage. It went very slowly and Jack watched through the passing beams of white iron work as the North Forty began to spread before him. To his right was the crater rim. The Chute was just in front of them and to their left the Caller stood on the plateau, vibrating steadily.

Several minutes later they arrived at the airlock hatch. As Tiller keyed in the code on an external panel to open it, Jack felt the entire Barn swaying slightly. The hatch opened and the elevator went the final ten feet into the sealed chamber.

They depressurized and stepped through into the changing area. They helped remove each other's suit helmets and gloves and entered the small, cockpit-like room that was the Barn's control area. Tiller placed the detonation suitcase he had carried on the counter beside one of the large portholes.

Looking out, Jack could see the entire area clearly. From this high vantage point, it became obvious why it was chosen. It was the perfect combination of geographical and man-made features for what the men had to accomplish. The climb up the far side of the crater rim would be perfect to slow down Moonmare, and the Chute leading down into the Corral would place her right in front of them. The pattern of charges he and Tiller had placed there over the last few days were positioned perfectly. If she got through them without setting one off by herself it would be a miracle.

As Tiller got the detonation system ready, Jack and Ericson established radio control and verified Polling's position.

"You up there, Pinto?" Ericson asked.

"Riding high and about to come overhead," Polling said.

"What do you say we lock in with some of those high tech lenses of yours," Ericson said.

"You got it."

From Polling's orbit, the North Forty was an oval pinpoint of light far in front of her on a vast expanse of darkness. Had she not had the proper grids and the laser guidance system she would never have even known it was there. As it was, however, she was able to lock in, as Ericson had said, and position his gear to record the event.

She first keyed in the grid coordinates and told the memory laser system on board to lock the appropriate cameras on that spot. Then, with a series of zooms, she was able to bring the area into view on the monitors in front of her. They were also being recorded at Ericson's location, and before the eyes of Pike and Balk.

At first the pinpoint of light became a tiny pin head sized oval. After several more zooms and grid adjustments, it was visible as an elongated dime-sized area with tiny hints of objects on it. "How's that?" Polling asked.

"Wonderful," Ericson said.

"Let's get to the *long* lens," Polling said. She adjusted the camera with its longest focal length, zoomed, and zoomed again. She then adjusted the coordinates again and zoomed a final time.

The dime had become a quarter, then a fifty cent piece. Finally, it was the size of a large egg. On the monitor before the men was now a distant but nearly perfect view of the North Forty in which the individual structures, though still very small, could be seen in some detail.

"Fantastic," Ericson said. "Just lock her right there and put her on auto."

Polling keyed in those instructions. From that point forward all cameras were slaved to the one they had just fine tuned. The system was locked in. Polling peered into the darkness on the far side of the crater rim adjacent to the Barn. She could see nothing. But she knew Moonmare was there — now very close, only minutes from coming over the top.

She had sensed another change. It had begun with the drop in intensities, the shifting of dominances in the parts of her dark existence, the confusion and, of course, the momentary peace and rest that came with these events.

These things were all familiar.

But when the fear had started again from the same place she was puzzled.

This was different.

No new threat. No new direction of escape had arisen.

Perhaps the answer was still before her.

Again, in a primitive way, along with the horror, a sense of renewed hope began to surface inside her.

She had gone on again, without question, her exhausted limbs aching as she slowly climbed a dark, powdery incline. And now, on the far side of the crater rim, the light was there. Something she had never experienced in the lunar darkness. It was close and more than a blush. It cast a warm, orange glow just beyond a wall of darkness, a light that called her and told her she was nearing home.

FORTY-FOUR

The charges were armed, the cameras were in place and recording. The Caller was working perfectly, sending its horrific, rhythmic vibrations into the lunar soil. The ETA clock said two minutes. The Barn control room swayed and shuddered with vibrations from the Mare's thunderous hoof beats.

It was time.

———————

In the darkness, Muriel felt herself drifting closer to something she had needed for years — something warm and comfortable. Some undulating wash of peace and forgiveness. In one part of her mind she knew what it was, but she could not quite unlock that vault of memory. That was okay, though, because now she knew things would be right. She would be released. Her life would finally be as it should.

———————

Moonmare began to crest the rim.

Her head appeared at first as a pale, momentary flash in the darkness beyond the crater rim. Then it flashed again and slowly came into view, bobbing forward and back, straining atop her long white neck.

Neither Jack nor Tiller were ready for what they saw. Her face was massive and horribly deformed. She had a thin mat of black, patchy hair and no suggestion of ears. Her nose consisted of two holes — one larger than the other — on a lump at the low center of her face. Beneath this she had no real mouth, but an indention that appeared to be a sagging, partially formed opening. Her skin had a shiny, almost greasy reddish tint between large, splotchy, pale areas. These were crisscrossed just beneath the surface with dark clusters of spidery veins. She had two eyes, but one was very large, bulging and sagging onto her cheek while the other was much smaller, appearing almost normal. Despite these deformities, it was obvious she was horrified, and even worse than the terrible misery and the grotesque individual features of her face, there were two overriding tragedies about her. She appeared to be a fetal organism and there was no doubt whatsoever — she had human genes.

"Oh, Jesus Christ," Jack blurted out.

Tiller went white. His jaw dropped. "She's...She's a fuckin' *baby*, Jack!"

She kept coming, now fully cresting the crater rim, bobbing and tossing her frightened, confused head in the stars.

Moments later her full body became visible.

The genes of a zebra were definitely there, but horribly distorted. Her frame was squat and blubbery with large lumps of quivering flesh and patches of hair growing from all parts of her body. Under her neck was a long, dangling, loose clump of reddish flesh, flapping as she moved. Her back was lumpy. It had what looked like the appearance of a zebra's stripes, but they were broken up and appeared rotted and scarred. Her skin was mostly pale, and translucent in some spots, showing through to dark vein clusters and internal organs. She had four thick legs on tremendous black hooves, and the stump of what looked like a tiny human arm protruding from the side of her shoulder. She had no tail.

FORTY-FIVE

From his position overhead, Polling could make her out, but in no detail. She appeared as a tiny horse-like figure with the suggestion of a striped back and a wide stomach bulging out on both of sides of her slow galloping figure.

And Ericson, it turned out, was suddenly left with only the same view.

In his control room something strange happened the moment Moonmare's head had begun to bob above the crater rim. Just before it had come into view, nearly all of the engineer's TV monitors and every one of his audio links to Jack and Tiller had suddenly gone dead. All that remained of his entire control system was the overhead telephoto lens shots from Pinto, and the audio link to Polling.

Stunned and utterly baffled, he whispered, "Oh my God! No! No! Not now!" and immediately began frantic attempts to right the system.

He could only attribute a massive failure like this to a freak power outage, but at Saltridge that was virtually impossible. All systems had multiple built-in redundancies, surge protectors and wiring to back-up generators, to protect against just such an event. And why were a few systems still on and others completely out? He tried the emergency reset buttons, the computer's re-boot commands, toggles, activation sequences, the emergency telephone, the speakers.

Nothing worked.

Later he would be told the failure had been a major system breaker failure — a freak overload caused by a tremendous, but unknown, surge of power sent through the entire Saltridge facility. And in spite of regularly scheduled testing, the generator system had failed to come on line. Being the dedicated and patriotic professional he was, he would believe this.

On the moon, Jack had heard the background static suddenly click to dead silence as Ericson's audio connection went dead. "Bill?" he said. "Bill, you there?"

At first he, too, was puzzled. Then, with Moonmare before him and the addition of this final, deadly piece of the puzzle, suddenly it began to make sense. Balk! He was controlling everything. He had planned all of this. He and Weincamp had played God. Somehow the doctor had included human genetic material and created a partially human mutation to wander, alone and horrified, in the lunar emptiness. Now Balk was making absolutely sure no possible trace of Moonmare or his connection to the project would remain as a skeleton in his political closet.

The wonderful darkness drifted closer to Muriel and now surrounded her with the first warmth she had felt in a very long time. Then it began to move inside her. Somehow it was filling her with a wonderful sense of renewal and well-being. It moved in and out of her mind and body, gently ebbing and flowing, warm then cool, modulating gracefully with the incredible peace that was now becoming a part of her mind and body.

FORTY-SIX

Moonmare began moving straight down the Chute toward the Corral. Jack looked at Tiller. The Texan seemed to be in a trance. His hand was moving slowly, hesitantly toward the "IGNITE" buttons.

Moonmare entered the Corral.

Jack winced, waiting for one of her hooves to ignite one of the charges. She moved in and among them, but miraculously, there was no explosion.

Just then something else happened.

Just as Tiller's hand poised to hit the deadly buttons, Moonmare suddenly stopped in her tracks.

———◆———

Something more had come to Muriel in the darkness. She realized it was different from the warmth and cool – it was alive. Needing and familiar, it hovered inside her. It began speaking to her in its own non-language, and Muriel began to weep quietly. It told her the time had come to release the guilt that had hovered so long in her mind. It said that she was a good woman and it had loved her for all time. It told her she was beautiful and she deserved, and would finally have, the happiness she so desired. She realized what it was — her soul — the part of her the terrifying dreams had taken away.

Jack looked to his left. In the distance he could see that the Caller had failed again — or had Balk shut it down?

Jack wasn't sure, but for some reason it didn't matter. He felt glad. And what he now saw in Moonmare supported that gladness, but also sent a dagger of sorrow through his heart. Her features changed radically. In that single instant since the Caller had failed, her grotesque, horrified face lost all its terrible misery and fear. It became the innocent, deformed face of a confused, deformed infant.

Jack saw no intelligence in her eyes, but he did see a hint of awareness, a questioning. It seemed she was somehow hopeful, asking anyone or anything, *Is it done now? Is the horror over? Am I now allowed to be whatever I am — at peace?*

Jack knew at that moment that he could not be a part of this child's murder.

Tiller's hand was poised over the buttons and he was about to push one. Jack held his arm. "No, Al." he said calmly, "She's a baby. We can't."

Tiller was confused and conflicted. He tried to pull away from Jack. Jack held firm.

FORTY-SEVEN

In the control room several floors down from Ericson, John Pike looked at Martin Balk and shook his head. Balk chuckled.

"...shame," he said.

The Vice President made a gesture and Pike slid back two separate panel covers under which were two buttons. One was labeled "ARM and the other was labeled "IGNITE". Above the two switches were the red letters "NUC".

"Okay, we're almost there." Balk said. "Let's arm."

Pike pushed the "ARM" button. It lit up and a warning message began to blink above the panel. "Extreme Caution. Nuclear weapon armed!"

Jack spoke calmly to Tiller. "Al, listen to me. We've been lied to. She's partially human and she's a child.

That's why Weincamp is dead. That's why Balk wants Moonmare wiped off the face of creation."

Tiller was shaking, unsure.

Jack looked deep into the Texan's eyes. "We're already dead, Al... We can't take her soul to our graves."

Tiller froze, staring into Jack's eyes, and Jack smiled reassuringly. He knew that this man, rough and proud and rugged as he was, also had a good heart.

He couldn't do it either.

———————

Ericson continued his frantic but futile attempts to reset his systems. He re-tried boot sequences and power ups. He tried the phone again but it remained dead. He leaped out of his chair and started to run out of the room in search of help, when the shot from Polling's camera suddenly changed.

———————

At that moment, realizing that Tiller might not fire the charges in the Corral, Balk gave a signal and Pike pressed another button on his control panel labeled "UMB". As Pike carried out the command, the transmitter at Saltridge went dead. The beam was cut.

Moonmare shuddered and convulsed. She stumbled, regained her balance for a moment, then went to her front knees. She tried desperately to regain her feet, but her extremities would not work properly.

Her neck swayed and twisted, quivering with spasms.

Her face convulsed and twitched.

Though she had no mouth, she appeared to be choking, gasping for a breath of air that in this world did not exist. Thick, dark liquid began to run from her eye sockets. She shuddered, tried once more to regain her feet, and rolled onto her side. Two explosive charges went off simultaneously directly beneath her. Her body was torn open and lifted off the lunar surface as if she had experienced a tremendous muscle spasm.

At first there was terror and confusion. But not the kind she had become so familiar with. Not the threat of attack. Something had left her. Some nurturing element that had been a critical part of her existence had suddenly been taken away. This realization surged throughout her body in waves of convulsive panic, and then she was twisting, reaching, frantically grasping, to retrieve her stolen soul.

Moments later, she felt her darkness being violently ripped apart and she understood that she would die. In that instant the panic and fear were swept away. There was no more pain, no more horror, no longing. She knew that was over now, and she had finally discovered something.

She had been right.

The release she had longed for had been here all along. She had no words for it, no way to describe it, but it was with her now, surrounding her, holding her in the final moments of her life.

FORTY-EIGHT

In Muriel's darkness, at that same moment, an exchange took place.

A gift was given.

A terrible wrong was made right.

A very long journey came to an end, and even in her deep sedated sleep, Muriel was aware of it.

———

It was then that Balk gave the order and Pike pushed the final button.

———

Janice Polling and Bill Ericson got their final shock of the mission when a nuclear fireball engulfed a segment of the moon reaching far beyond the limits of the

North Forty, and everything in that small piece of lunar acreage was instantly vaporized.

Bill Ericson stopped trying to right the system. He sat frozen in his seat. Then, realizing it was too late and his efforts had failed, he whispered, "Dear God!," dropped his head into his hands and began to sob.

He would remain convinced for some time that had power not failed he would have somehow been able to avert what he was later told was an accidental discharge of the nuclear device.

FORTY-NINE

Seventeen days later, Muriel Olsen stepped into Jack Moore's apartment with Callisto on a leash at her side. She placed a newspaper on the kitchen table. The issue was four days old. It had one front page story that Muriel had read many times over and another she hadn't yet noticed.

The story of interest to Muriel read:

TEST PILOTS CRASH
The crash of a prototype S-221 stealth fighter cost the lives of two veteran test pilots today, according to an official military spokesperson.
Killed were Air Force Colonel Allan F. Tiller and Lieutenant Colonel John D. Moore.
Captain Damian S. Parker, Air Force public affairs specialist, said the crash occurred during a series of routine, low altitude, high speed, night flights over the southern California desert.

"We fly these state of the art aircraft at speeds of up to mach four over uneven desert terrain in order to put their technical capabilities to the maximum test," Parker said. "It's extremely dangerous work, but it is also indispensable in maintaining our national security."

Evidently, the craft struck the side of a rock face at maximum speed. The impact was reported to be so great that the entire craft and its contents were instantly vaporized.

"While technical and design problems are always a concern with prototype aircraft," Parker said, "and these men were two of our top pilots, we think that in this case the accident was due to a loss of orientation during a series of rapid and complicated maneuvers. Moore was at the controls and from what we were able to hear in a radio message recorded seconds before the accident, it seems he had become disoriented at a critical moment."

Parker went on to say the Air Force would mourn the loss of two of its finest. "These two officers were tops in their field," he told reporters. "We are all shocked and terribly saddened at their loss."

Though the cause of the accident seems apparent, a full investigation is now underway by a team of military flight experts.

The second headline, the one that Muriel hadn't yet discovered, read:

METEOR IMPACT SHAKES LUNAR BACKSIDE

What scientists believe was the impact of a large meteor was recorded by seismic monitoring devices three days ago on the far side of the moon.

Initial reports place the impact in a north-western section of Mare Moscoviense, a large flat area mapped by previous lunar flights but — since the lunar globe rotates at the same rate as its revolutions around the earth — perpetually hidden from our eyes.

The impact has evidently caused a series of quakes on the moon which have been calculated at roughly the equivalent of an 9.0 earthquake. The quakes have been noted by British, French, German and Russian scientists, as well.

There has been a vaguely stated, and as yet unclear cover up, rumor leveled by Iran against the United States regarding the three day period during which the impact was kept classified by the U.S. government.

Involvement in the incident, however, by the U.S. or any other country has been called nonsense by the Administration's Press Secretary, Daniel Mead.

"We're sure it's nothing more than the impact of one heck of a large meteor," Mead told reporters at an early morning press conference, "but we're monitoring the situation on a twenty-four hour basis. Any speculation that the United States has in any way caused or been a party to some aspect of this incident is totally unfounded and ridiculous."

Muriel looked around.

The apartment was just as she had seen it on her last visit with Jack. Nothing had changed.

Sunlight was falling on the living room couch. Cal left Muriel's side and wandered toward it. He hopped up onto the cushion and began to sniff and circle, deciding on a spot to lie down.

The German clock was keeping perfect time, as usual. The models of jets and the computer books were on the shelves and countertops just as Jack had left them. Slowly, lovingly, she looked over and touched everything in the living room. The lamp, a cup, the television, a dictionary, the clock. As she did this she visualized Jack touching each item. She imagined how he used or needed it, or how he talked about it, or how it made him happy.

When there was nothing left in the living room, she moved to the bathroom and did the same thing. His razor, the towel still hanging over the shower door, the mirror with his fingerprints, the tile floor, the walls.

Muriel did this in every room in Jack's apartment and it took her nearly an hour. The last place she visited was the den he used as a home office. His desk was still spread with papers, the pens and opened manuals. His computer was still on.

She sat down and looked at the ASNAi logo. There was a choice for e-mail. She remembered the morning she had stood behind him watching him excitedly receive his own e-mailed letter. She opened the program browser, found the iMuriel folder and opened it. She then returned to the e-mail program, entered the two codes and slowly navigated though the access sequence. A menu came up — a mailbox. It asked of her, "Check Mail?" She keyed in "Y".

It said there was a letter in the secret buffer. She asked to read it. She keyed the remaining secret codes. The envelope came forward, the letter unfolded.

It was from Jack.

It began:

My Dearest Muriel,
I love you. I love you. I will always love you and I am so
sorry for having left you without a word!

Writing from Saltridge. Must hurry. Will place this in
buffer for delivery later. If not home to receive it myself, hope to
God you find it. Print a copy and deliver it anonymously to a
man named Samuel Morris, publisher of the World View Moni-
tor. Also deliver a copy to Bill Ericson on Sanders Court in the
White Palm Condo complex.

Suspect murder, inhumane activities, and an illegal gov-
ernment cover up on the mission am involved in. Following are
the names, dates, and facts that I know of, and my suspicions....

As she continued to read, Cal hopped down off
the couch and walked into the den. He paused, yawned,
and curled up in the dusty sunlight on the carpet by the
sliding glass door.

THE END